I S.P.I.

Supernatural Paranormal Investigations

Spicy Sorcery

I0602003

Michelle Lee

BLUE FORGE PRESS

Port Orchard · Washington

I S.P.I. Spicy Sorcery (Volume 2)
Copyright February 2023
by Michelle Lee

First Print Edition, February 2023
First eBook Edition, February 2023

ISBN 978-1-59092-975-9

Cover and interior design by Brianne DiMarco

For information about film, reprint or other subsidiary rights, contact blueforgegroup@gmail.com

This is a work of fiction. Names, characters, locations, and all other story elements are the product of the authors' imaginations and are used fictitiously. Any resemblance to actual persons, living or dead, or other real life situations is purely coincidental.

Blue Forge Press is the print division of the volunteer-run, federal 501(c)3 nonprofit company, Blue Forge Group, founded in 1989 and dedicated to bringing light to the shadows and voice to the silence. We strive to empower storytellers across all walks of life with our four divisions: Blue Forge Press, Blue Forge Films, Blue Forge Gaming, and Blue Forge Records. Find out more at www.BlueForgeGroup.org

Blue Forge Press
7419 Ebbert Drive Southeast
Port Orchard, Washington 98367
blueforgepress@gmail.com
360-550-2071 ph.txt

For Tina, Auntie Bev, Kristen, Lisa and my mom. (It was her idea to be a witch, not mine, just want to make that clear. She made me revise the story to make her more devious.) I love you, Mom.

Spicy Sorcery

❧

Michelle Lee

Book 6
Witch Recipes

Chapter One

Not even twenty-four hours after rescuing a real live purple people eater and sending her back to her realm, I was standing behind my desk facing Mick, the alpha of the wolf pack. Not to mention one of the sexiest men alive. He was staring me down.

Me, Risa Sanders, owner of I S.P.I. and the one and only supernatural, paranormal, investigator, unmistaken badass female, getting intimidated by the oversized testosterone-laden shifter; this would never do.

"Mick, sit your fine ass down," I snapped.

The smirk on Mick's face let me know that the fine part was vocalized and not silently thought as I had intended. Damn this man for getting me flustered. He'd licked my blood off my abdomen yesterday. My brain still cemented the feel of his tongue in the front of my mind.

"I'm a gentleman. I'm waiting for your perfectly round and fine ass to sit first," Mick drawled.

Danny, I reminded myself. *You are in a relationship with Danny; this man is off-limits.* Honestly, it wasn't going to matter what I told myself. Mick sent my hormones into overdrive every single time I was around him.

My hands fumbled around behind, tugging my chair closer, and I lowered myself, keeping my eyes on Mick. Where my cheeks were expecting to sit on the cushioned seat, they only met air, and my downward trajectory continued. The demon chair had moved by itself.

I landed with a painful unladylike oomph, and I think I even bounced a little, much to my humiliation. Beyond caring, I adjusted the girls from their zippy recoil while Mick's eyes bored a hole right through my top.

A string of vigorously colorful language spewed from my lips in a bout of verbal diarrhea as I got to my feet and forcefully yanked the damn chair into place and planted my perfectly round and fine ass to use Mick's words right into the seat. I ignored the cylinder groaning out the word *bitch.* To my shame, there was a moment where I wished I had gas.

"Nice show, Risa," Mick chuckled as he sat down. "Pick up your tits, and let's get to business."

I glanced down at my chest to make sure the girls were in place. "Why are you here? I'm supposed to be on vacation."

Mick leaned forward, "Yet you still found time to create a ruckus and smuggle out a purple people eater. We both know the vacation is a sham."

I scoffed, "It wasn't. Jonielle needed help, and I felt a connection to her. I don't owe you an explanation." I crossed my arms, growing irritated. "What do you want?"

"Maggie," Mick imitated my pose. "I know she's alive. Your friend caught the scent, and so did I. It's been three weeks now since she disappeared. I'm willing to hire you since your solve rate is perfect. I'm man enough to admit I need help."

Mick was man enough for a lot of things, was the thought that flitted through my head. I sighed, hoping it stayed in my head and not slip off my tongue as he brought that out in me. "I already told you that I'd help you. Whatever this is," I gestured at him, "isn't necessary."

That smirk that tempted me to slap it off his face, or climb him like I was a monkey, came across his face again.

"I'm making it official, Risa. I need you."

Oh, damn. Those three little words about had me ready to peel my clothes off. I think I was panting. Were my pants wet? What the hell was happening right now? It had to be a dream.

Mick threw his head back and laughed a big belly laugh. "Woman, you kill me."

I was the color of an overripe tomato. All those words had come out of my mouth. "Damn it! Stop flustering me!" I shouted to cover my embarrassment.

Mick leaned forward again, so close I could feel his minty breath on my flaming hot cheeks. "I'll know the moment you are single, and we will have an entirely different conversation then. I can guarantee you'll be talking to God."

If my office door hadn't opened at that precise moment, I'd have jumped him. His effect on me was that potent. Probably because I knew I couldn't have him now that I was in a relationship. Regardless, Mick stood gracefully and gave a bow to the woman who'd walked in before he made his exit.

Chapter Two

That man is certainly a walking sex symbol," the woman replied, staring after Mick. "You should test those waters. By that, I mean sleep with him."

I couldn't disagree. "How can I help you?" I politely asked, giving her a quick once over.

My senses told me the lady was magical, though she didn't carry herself as if she were. Short, probably only five feet tall, dark hair, olive skin, and an open, friendly face. It made me want to call her mom and tell her that man was teasing me. I blinked slowly, hoping my mind would clear.

"I've never gone to a private investigator before," the woman cautioned me as she took a seat in a questionable old chair. "Maybe I'd feel more at ease if you told me a little about yourself while you ate a cookie."

I took the proffered cookie, and I suddenly found myself telling this woman about my three sons, Danny, Mick, and my problems with my exes. What the hell was that? I zipped my lips and stared at the cookie with suspicious eyes—devious woman.

"What brings you here?" I asked again, pushing the remains of the truth serum cookie out of the way.

"My name is Nina, and I need some help," Nina told me. "Obviously, or why would I be here talking to you, right? Silly me. I'm nervous."

"No need to be," I tried to reassure her. "Why don't

you tell me about the problems you are having that brought you here?"

"It would make sense that I tell you that, wouldn't it?" Nina fidgeted. "I think someone is trying to scare me out of town or something."

I leaned my elbows on the desk and studied the nervous woman. Nina wasn't dishonest or evasive; she was genuinely concerned. "Do you feel like you are in danger?"

"I don't know," Nina slowly answered. She drew in a deep exaggerated breath, then let loose. "I own a business and a food truck. My business is making healthy and balanced meals for people that are too busy to cook or who can't cook. I take my food truck out and deliver them and sell lunch while I do that. I love making food. It nourishes people, makes them happy, and soothes the soul."

I glanced at the cookie sitting next to me; it made sense, I guess. Something niggled at the back of my mind. "My son is a chef, as I told you, I can understand that. But what's the problem?"

"I think someone is sabotaging my food. Or my garden. I'm not quite sure. People are acting weird after they eat my food. It's amusing to get proposed to by strangers. You know how some people really love certain foods and go crazy over them? That's what I thought it was. Then about two months ago, my garden started growing so fast that it was like someone was putting some serious fertilizer on it. I remember thinking that was some powerful cow shit," Nina exclaimed.

That little thought in the back of my mind grew more prominent the more Nina talked, and I began to feel a kinship with her. "Okay, someone was tinkering with your harvest," I made a note on the pad of paper I'd pulled out. "People acting crazy over your food."

"I think crazy is an understatement in some cases,"

Nina clarified. "There are times when people get downright aggressive with wanting more."

"Is it certain food only?" I glanced at the truth cookie again. "Like cookies?"

"What?" Nina gave me a confused look. "I don't remember any specific recipe. I make different things all the time. I don't necessarily use any recipe at all."

Then it hit me—kitchen witch. Nina was a kitchen witch, with possibly some earth magic infused in there. Did she not know? How is that possible? I *know* it's likely because that happened to me, but I felt my magic coming in, and all sorts of things started happening, including my hair spontaneously changing colors with my moods.

"Are those the only things you've noticed? The garden and people reacting to your recipes?" I asked, tapping my pen on the pad of paper.

"Yeah, and I'm worried that someone is doing something to my garden. Spiking the plants with drugs or something? Injecting meth?" Nina worried her hands. "I can afford to pay for your services if that is what you are worried about."

"It's not," I quickly replied. To cover my blunder, I pulled out a contract and slid it across the desk to Nina. "Fill that out. It explains my fees."

Nina glanced at it briefly, scrawled her signature on the bottom line, then went back up and filled in her address information and pushed it back at me. I picked it up and looked at the address. It was on the border of Glimmering Rock and Branstone. Interesting.

It didn't give me one iota of a clue if she knew about magical beings or not. I was positive she was one and unclear on if she knew it or not. I also had a sneaking suspicion that something else was going on other than her natural skills coming through her cooking.

"Is there any competition for you?" I asked

thoughtfully.

"Food trucks? Sure, there are a ton of them," Nina waved her hand carelessly. "Locally, there isn't any other home delivery service like I do. There are large businesses that do it, but I don't mail my meals. I hand-deliver them the same day I make them."

"Sounds fantastic," I sighed dramatically. "I *can* cook. I just don't. My son Gage usually delivers food to me throughout the week or has one of his brothers do it to make sure I'm eating something other than processed food."

"I'd be happy to make you a couple of meals," Nina told me with enthusiasm. "I love taking care of people."

"Are any of your other family members cooks? Is that where you learned it?" I asked out of curiosity.

"I think my family has an affinity for cooking and baking. My mother is quite a wonderful cook," Nina answered with a smile.

It stands to reason that somewhere down the line someone knew they were kitchen witches. I wasn't going to mention it until I knew where she stood on the whole subject matter. "I bet you had fun cooking with her when you were a kid," I replied wistfully. I had some of those memories with my mom, but she wasn't all that skilled in the kitchen.

"Tell you what," Nina sat forward. "If you can solve this case for me in under a week, I'll bring you meals two times a week for a month. If you are happy with the food, you can spread the word about me. In the meantime, you can have these cookies."

"Deal," I stuck my hand out quickly. It shouldn't take me any time at all to find out if someone was intentionally sabotaging this sweet woman. The offer of good food was too much to pass up. "I'll come out to your place in the morning and look around."

16

Chapter Three

I walked Nina outside and came to a screeching halt at the sight of my Jeep sitting there with Mick leaning up against it looking all smug. I'd taken the bus to get to my office this morning. That's how I was planning to get home until now.

My Jeep had rolled yesterday after a magical attack blasted us on our way to Ivan's for Jonielle to escape. I suspected that Wiley was behind the assault, but I couldn't prove it yet.

Nina nudged me in the side several times and gave me a knowing wink. "You should handle him," she told me. I wasn't sure about that, and I was too involved with another man to find out. "He'd be a fun romp."

"My boyfriend might object," I told Nina with a weak smile. Her goading wasn't helping my willpower.

Mick only raised his eyebrows and crossed his arms over the burly chest I wanted to sink my teeth into; who was I kidding? I wanted to take a bite out of several areas on that man. Nina patted my arm sympathetically and strolled over to her car, looking her fill at the alpha wolf.

"Tell me she brought you food," Mick righted himself as I walked over to him.

"You know her?" I couldn't hide the surprise in my voice if I'd wanted to.

"Yeah. Nina lives near the bar, delivers food to a couple of my pack, and her food truck makes the rounds," Mick furrowed his brows at me. "Did you not know her?"

"No," I muttered and pushed him out of the way. "Did you fix my Jeep? How much do I owe you?"

"Nothing," Mick gave me a strange look. "We only pulled out a few dents. Otherwise, she's solid." He held out the keys to me. "You can either give me a ride back, or I'll shift and run there."

I snatched the keys dangling from his hand and, with no shame, leaned forward and planted a kiss on the frame of my Jeep. "My baby," I crooned. "Get in. I'll drop you off."

Mick was shaking his head as he rounded the Jeep in climbed into it. "Does Danny know he's competing with your Jeep?"

I huffed in indignation, but he wasn't totally off the mark with his comment. "She's been with me for a long time. Danny is recent and can hold his own against a magical attack."

Mick snorted. "If longevity is the key to unlocking the hotness, you've known me quite a while, and yet the Jeep still got further than I have."

"The Jeep isn't an asshole," I retorted hotly. "You don't want me." I regretted it the moment it left my lips. His answering growl was enough to push all the libido buttons.

"Don't speak for me, woman," Mick finally ground out, bristling. "Is Nina okay? She's in my territory, and I keep an eye on her. Nina has phenomenal sass."

"Does she know she's a witch?" I blurted out.

"Yes and no," Mick answered without giving me a solid answer. "She thinks all the magic stuff is made up but wants it to be real. She's been told she's a witch, and she laughs at it like it's a joke."

18

"Well, doesn't that just make things so much easier?" I muttered. I didn't tell him any more, and we drove in silence. Pulling up to his bar, I turned to look at him. "Thanks for bringing my Jeep to me and pulling out the dents. I truly appreciate it."

Mick's eyes raked over my face, making it heat under the intensity of his stare. "You're welcome," he answered with a husky tone. "I can still taste you."

Damn it if I didn't bite my tongue. Mick grinned and got out, gently closing the door. "Watch yourself, woman. It does something to my wolf to see you injured."

I waved hello to Crowley, a medium and seer who had a billiards addiction, then backed out and headed home. I was brooding about the mixed signals from Mick. He was a complication I wasn't ready to deal with, and I had to keep reminding myself about Danny.

I don't even know why I was stumbling over the situation at all; Mick was a man whore. He didn't do girlfriends or dating. Part of me felt tempted to give in and sample the goods and move on like I used to do. Get it out of my system and all that. Only I didn't think it would turn out that way.

I drove home and sat down at my computer to start doing some searches on food trucks in the area to get an idea of who Nina's competition was. I also looked up gardeners as I knew there was a very competitive market for award-winning produce. Some of those people were crazy.

I spent a couple of hours at it, came up with a shortlist, and did basic searches. I wasn't sure I was on the right track with my train of thought, so I didn't bring Danny in on it. Plus, I wasn't supposed to be working either. I was supposed to be drinking mystery potions to help me get a handle on my magic.

Gage, my middle son, the chef, had told me that I

needed someone to train me. Most likely, it was true. When I was little, I trained with my parents, and they eventually gave up because I didn't show an affinity for magic. Boy, did that change. I practically bled it now. That led to thinking of Nina not knowing about her status.

My guess was she was infusing her garden and food with magic. If that was the case, she should have zero competition. A kitchen witch had no equal when they put their talents to use creating recipes. It could also make Nina deadly as hell.

I glanced at my phone and made a snap decision to call Gage. He picked up after the fourth ring. "Mom? Is everything okay?"

"Yeah, honey, I'm fine. Do you know a local home chef named Nina?" I chanced the question.

"Everyone knows Nina," Gage sighed in relief. "I try to copy her dishes all the time, but I always fall short of the mark, even when she gives me the recipe."

I couldn't help myself; I laughed. "Nina's a kitchen witch, honey. Don't tell her that I told you that. *You* can try calling her that and see if she reacts and then let me know."

There was silence on the other end of the phone from my middle son. "Kitchen witch, why didn't I see that? I wonder if she'd come work for me. Wait, does she know you are my mother?"

"Nina knows I have a son who is a chef. I didn't give her your name. Why would that matter?" I asked, suddenly confused.

"Because you said not to tell Nina you told me that," Gage repeated. "Are you working on a case for her? Is Nina okay?"

"Yes, Nina hired me. I'm not telling you any more than that. Do you know anyone that has a grudge against her?" I tried.

"Every insecure chef out there," Gage threw out. "I don't believe any of it is genuine hate; it's pure jealousy. Her sarcasm is on point, too."

"Thanks, honey." I was going to trail Nina tomorrow. I wouldn't tell her that, though. I wanted to get a good idea of reactions to her without people thinking they were being watched. "Have a good night."

"Find a trainer, Mom," Gage reminded me before hanging up.

Chapter Four

I woke up with my mind racing in different directions. Scenarios were playing on a reel of ways that an unknowing kitchen witch could harm people. I doubted that was the case with Nina, but you never know. What if someone seriously pissed her off while she was making their food? She could put those emotions into the recipe, and the person eating it would suffer the consequences.

Talk about an untraceable crime. It was brilliant in a convoluted way. I'd have to carefully word my questions because I didn't want Nina to think she was harming people. That same train of thought made me want to give those truth cookies to Mick.

I could have Nina make a gnarly recipe to feed the new town criminal, Wiley, that would give away his hidden nature. That thought had merit. Nina was mischievous enough to do it, too; that was easy enough to see.

Focus, Risa, I reminded myself. I had Nina's case to figure out and do it quickly to get some of the delightful food she makes. I shook my head. I'd do damn near anything for good food except cook for myself.

I rolled out of bed and started getting ready for my morning. First, Nina's house, then covertly follow her around and see if I could spy anything out of the ordinary. It sounded simple to me, though, with my track record, simple could turn into complicated in a matter of seconds.

I made myself a cup of coffee and poured it into my to-go cup, gathered my purse, notebook, keys, and headed out to my Jeep. Words couldn't express my gratitude to Mick for rescuing my baby and making sure she still ran. I skimmed my fingers over her red paint, murmuring words of love. Yes, I was that person.

I looked at the piece of paper that I had written Nina's address on and headed in that direction. With any luck, she'd be in the middle of making something delicious, and I'd get to be her taste tester. A girl could hope, at least. That was my rationalization for not eating something for breakfast. It had nothing to do with the lack of motivation for cooking, I swear.

I couldn't even think that with a straight face. Not to mention that anyone who knew me wouldn't believe that. I was startled out of my thoughts by the sudden ringing of my phone. I glanced down and saw my oldest son's name on the screen; I winced and reached for the phone, expecting some sort of bad news.

"Hi, Gavin. What's up?" I answered the call.

"Hi, Mom. You left me a message about a new office chair. Is something wrong with yours? I know it's old, but I got told it was spelled to remain in good working order so it wouldn't need to be replaced," Gavin told me.

"Who told you that?" That was the first I'd heard that tidbit of information.

"Luca," Gavin replied a little too innocently. "He's the one who brought the chair to me to give you. Luca said you wouldn't accept a gift from him. He's right; you wouldn't have," he pointed out, not helpfully.

"There's a reason for that," I muttered. "Yeah, hon, I need a new chair. Preferably not one from Luca." Luca was Jameson's father, part demon, part angel. "That chair tries to injure me, and I was told there is some living entity in it."

There was a pregnant silence from Gavin on the other end of the phone while he processed that bit of information. "If that were true," he finally said, "don't you think Jameson would have noticed that?"

"Why would he? If Luca wasn't the one who spelled it, there is no reason for Jameson to catch on to it," I retorted hotly. "If you can't find me a new chair, I'll find one myself. I'm tired of getting thrown around my office in front of clients."

Gavin sighed theatrically. "I'll look around."

I hung up before I got angry with my son. There was way too much of his troll father in him. Of my three sons, Gavin was the one that tried my patience the most. It wasn't too much longer after I hung up that I arrived at Nina's house.

I didn't even need to look at the address. The food truck in the driveway gave it away. It made me snicker to see *Open Your Pie Hole* across the side of the vehicle. I was still chuckling as I opened my Jeep door, and the mouthwatering smells wafted past my nose. That was all it took as the scented air grabbed me by my nostrils, tickled my empty stomach, and dragged me to Nina's door.

A tall man answered my knock, gave me a small smile, and invited me in. "You must be Risa," the man said, closing the door behind me. "I'm Ed, Nina's husband. She's in the kitchen," he gestured down the hallway.

I didn't need directions; I followed the tantalizing smells. "Hi, Nina," I called out, startling her. "It smells like heaven in here."

I took in the large island in the center of the kitchen covered with produce, herbs, and other various ingredients. It was quite the production Nina had going on. The fact that she was using her own kitchen and not a commercial kitchen was impressive.

"Oh, Risa," Nina welcomed me in. "Thank you. I'm getting the meals ready to deliver after we get them packaged up. I'm making my chicken in a wine sauce with sauteed mushrooms. I already loaded up the truck with today's lunch ingredients. I'm going to do a traditional spaghetti and meatball dish, with some steamed broccoli, because people need their vegetables."

I swear my stomach growled loud enough for the neighbors to hear. I blushed and watched as she continued her cooking. Under the smell of sautéing garlic, I scented her magic at work. "Anything unusual happening today?" I asked, resisting the urge to dip my fingers in the frosting of the iced cake on the counter.

"Parts of the garden were messy like someone had been trying to dig up the plants," Ed offered.

Nina moved swiftly and handed me a muffin. "I baked those early this morning. Try it."

I wasn't about to argue. "Mind if I look at the garden?" I asked, forcing myself to unwrap the muffin slowly instead of stuffing the entire thing in my mouth.

"Not at all, I'm rather proud of it," Nina answered. "Ed, show Risa where it is."

I felt reasonably sure I'd be able to find it on my own, considering I could see it from the window, but I only opened my mouth to put more muffin in there and dutifully followed Ed outside to the flourishing garden. I suddenly felt like backtalking and sassing were not in my best interest—damn muffin. Nina's food was dangerous in an amusing way.

Chapter Five

Ed left me to my own devices out in the garden. I can only assume that someone irked Nina while making her muffins, perhaps letting their mouths get the best of them if my reticence about letting sarcasm fly was any indication. It certainly didn't stop me from eating the rest of the delicious muffin.

I wandered up and down the aisles of vegetables. It appeared that Nina could make anything grow. I plucked a berry from a bush and popped it in my mouth, then did the same with a snap pea and felt peace. I briefly wondered if she wanted to adopt me. I was centuries older than her, but she didn't need to know that.

I arrived at the location that looked tampered with and squatted down, my magic bristling under my skin. There was no question that something wasn't right here, and I got the sense that it was hazardous. If I was right, these were carrots in front of me. Next to those were the mushrooms Gage was always gushing about for his recipes. Morels or something like that.

I reached out to run my fingers over the leaves of the carrots, and before I could even touch the plant, my magic had me repelling. An awareness tingled over my skin, and I shot to my feet. Tampering, indeed. I think someone replaced the plants with something else.

Neither Ed nor Nina would suspect anything since it's in their backyard. They planted the plants, nurtured them, and harvested them. I wasn't positive that was what had happened, but if my magic reacted that strongly and I hadn't even touched the plant, something was wrong with it.

I ran through the garden as gently as I could, avoiding trampling on the plants, and flung the backdoor open, shouting, "Don't eat that!"

Nina had been about to pop a mushroom in her mouth. I've seen Gage do that countless times. He'd tell me that a good chef always tastes their food before considering it finished and ready to serve. "Why?" Nina asked, dropping the mushroom.

"I think the carrots and mushroom plants were switched," I blurted out. I had no idea what would have happened if Nina had eaten that. "Ed said it looked like someone had been digging up the plants, and I think that's what happened exactly."

Ed raised his eyebrows. "They looked the same, but I did notice the churned-up dirt."

"We didn't use any carrots today," Nina replied slowly. She turned to the refrigerator and pulled out a bowl of mushrooms. She picked one up and studied it carefully. "I didn't even notice this. You're right, Risa. These are fake morels. People could have gotten seriously sick from this or even died. It's a damn good thing I haven't added these to anything yet."

It was still sad to see Nina dump fabulous smelling food out, even if I didn't particularly care for mushrooms. Nina looked shaken and stood there for a moment, staring at nothing.

"You think the carrots, too, Risa?" Ed asked me.

I nodded. "My instincts kept me from touching

28

them, so I don't think going out there and yanking them from the ground would be a good idea. I get the feeling we shouldn't touch them."

"This is crazy," Nina finally said. "Did I tell you my daughter is an author? That sounds like something she would create in one of her stories."

I snickered again, "That about sums up my life. A crazy story."

"What looks like a carrot?" Ed wondered aloud.

"Hemlock," Nina responded absently. "Commonly known as hogweed. Good thing you didn't touch it."

How this woman didn't know she was a witch was beyond me. I was born to the magical life, as she was, but I was raised knowing it. Given that, you'd think I'd know more about things like hemlock, yet I didn't. For once, I was glad my magic interfered.

"We should probably check the blueberries, too," Nina told Ed. "Nightshade is often confused with blueberries."

What the hell? I was never eating anything out in the wild again. "Couldn't hurt," was my meek response. I followed them back out to the garden and trusted my magic to let me know if there was danger or not.

"Yes, the blueberries have been tampered with as well," Nina sighed. "Look, the berries are shiny, and the leaves are the wrong shape."

"Okay," I interrupted. "Have you had anyone report any illnesses to you after eating your food?"

"No," Nina fidgeted nervously. "Now I'm afraid to serve anyone food."

"What ingredients did you put in your truck? Anything from the garden?" I asked, looking between her and Ed.

"No. The sauce I made a couple of months ago and froze. Same with the meatballs. The garlic I harvested a

29

week ago. Oh, the broccoli, I did, but there isn't any poisonous plant I know of that looks like broccoli, so I think that is safe," Nina began to pace. "I can replace the mushrooms in today's dish with these other here."

Ed promptly bent over and picked a bunch of the mushrooms to bring in the house. I wondered if Danny was trainable like that? That thought immediately led to one that Mick in no way, shape, or form would be. Why that would matter, I couldn't say.

I think it was time for me to spill the beans about magic. I wasn't technically violating any rules since she had magic already. The knowledge she had about plants had to have gotten handed down through generations of witches in her family.

Rip the band-aid off, right? "Nina, you are a witch."

Ed merely rolled his eyes, cocked his head to the side, and gave me a strange look. Nina scoffed at me. "I'm not mean," she stated, slightly irritated. "I'm funny."

I fought back a laugh. "That's not what I meant. You have magic. You are what is called a kitchen witch. You are a real-life witch. Not a green-faced, warty nose, pointed hat wearing, cackling, and riding a broom cartoon character—a witch. I'm magic. That's how I sensed the poisonous plant."

Nina looked at me like I had grown three extra heads that sprouted unicorn horns and belched glittery cupcakes. "Magic isn't real," she spluttered.

I thought quickly, my mind racing. "When you made those muffins, were you irritated?"

"What does that have to do with anything?" Nina huffed, and Ed semi-snorted. "How did you know?"

"Because when I ate it, I had the sudden feeling that backtalking or sassing you would be a bad idea. Yesterday when I ate your cookie, it was like I swallowed a bottle of truth serum. When you cook, whatever emotion you are feeling is what gets put into your food," I declared, knowing the woman was going to think I'm insane.

I had to prove magic. And to do that, I needed to use mine. Typically, that had mixed results, especially with this newly blooming magic in its pubescent stage. Should I chance it? I didn't know. It was risky at best. At worst, I didn't want to contemplate what could happen.

"That's not true," Nina's voice held a note of hesitation in it.

"Magic is real, and unchecked, dangerous," I spouted. *Practice what you preach, Risa,* I told myself. I needed to find a trainer. "I'll prove it. Understand, I have no idea what will happen, so I'm going to apologize upfront. My magic is kind of going through some changes."

I went for a simple glamour and pictured my skin turning blue, so I looked like Jonielle, a friend I'd met not too long ago who was a purple people eater trying to get back to her realm. Without a mirror, I have no clue if it worked or not.

It became apparent something had changed because Ed began to blink slowly, and Nina gaped at me, her mouth trying to form words that wouldn't come. I let go of my magic and hoped, like mad, that I went back to normal.

"Why is your hair orange?" Nina finally spat out. She reached forward and yanked it as if I somehow put a wig on without her noticing.

I sighed. I walked over to the hemlock plant and reached for it again, letting my magic loose to protect me. Thin streams of flames shot from my fingers and incinerated the plant before our eyes.

I walked over to the blueberries, and this time the plant froze. I picked up a rock and shattered it. "See?" I wanted to be proud that I hadn't just burned down her garden, but I wisely kept that statement from spewing from my lips.

31

Nina swayed in place, and Ed reached out to steady her. "You forgot the morels," she told me pointedly, waiting for me to rid her garden of the poison. "Get to it."

Chapter Six

I should have realized that trying to explain to Nina how magic worked for her while cooking wasn't a good thing. As I sat there and watched people eat their spaghetti and meatballs in the park and become skeptical, astonished, and shocked, it dawned on me what was happening.

I made my way to the line of people waiting, and when I got to the window, I quietly suggested that Ed take over the cooking part since it was mainly boiling noodles and heating things. Nina looked out the window at the shocked people in the park and started to laugh.

"Well, I'm glad someone knows how I feel!" Nina declared but let Ed finish cooking the lunches. "At least they aren't punching each other, though it would be funny."

I didn't know if she believed me or not, but when I tried to explain how a kitchen witch could negatively affect people without understanding it, she had chuckled and asked if it worked that way if she was having dirty thoughts too. Mischievous was an understatement for this woman. I hadn't even gotten into the earth affinity part I believed she possessed with how she could grow things.

I walked back out to my hiding in plain sight spot and watched. The more significant problem was someone was intentionally trying to either hurt, kill, or sabotage Nina, or through her, the masses of people she served. I was hoping the culprit would be stupid enough to be watching.

I pulled out my phone and called Mick. "Hey," I greeted him when he answered gruffly. "Do you have a wolf good at surveillance available?"

"Depends. Are you paying? What's the job?" Mick barked out.

"I can pay a little. I was hoping someone would keep an eye on Nina's property for a couple of nights. I've found that someone is messing with her," I replied honestly. I gave him a brief rundown and clued him in that I spilled the beans about the magic.

Mick broke out in laughter. "How'd that go? You aren't the first to tell her."

I cleared my throat a little. "I, uh, had to prove magic was real," I admitted quietly. Mick was on the council and could find fault with what I had done. I needed to tread carefully.

"Fuck. Did you blow up her house?" Mick growled.

Letting out an aggravated huff, I responded, "No. Nothing bad happened."

"I'll ask one of the guys that get food from her, and he'll most likely do it for free. I'll let you know," Mick told me, cutting the conversation short.

I stared at my phone for a second, startled at the abrupt end. I got over it and called one of the witches specializing in protective wards and arranged for several to get placed around Nina's property, which should help with the intruders. Satisfied with that, I sat back to people watch again.

Everything seemed to be status quo until Nina started to pack things in and close down for the day. Then an agitated man approached the window and began to wave his arms about angrily. He wasn't speaking loud enough for me to hear him, so I got up and slowly made my way closer, trying to be stealthy.

Given the look on Nina's face, this dude had a death wish. I'd never quite seen someone's eyebrows do the devil look before, but Nina pulled it off without a hitch. I found myself hesitating on moving forward. Oh well, I was close enough to hear now.

"You are encroaching on my territory!" the angry little man was screeching.

"You don't own these streets," Nina pointed out caustically. "As you can well see, we are closing up for the day anyway. Take your complaints and deep fry them as you do with your food. Don't make me start sprinkling the F word on everything."

I swallowed a laugh at that comment, but the man didn't find it quite as amusing as I did. It seemed he had no sense of humor and sour taste to boot, considering his clothes didn't even match. It wasn't difficult to surmise that he was a competitor or trying to be.

"Be that as it may, my customers are still coming over here looking to buy from you instead of me!" the man bellowed.

"Improve your recipes then!" Nina shot back hotly. "That doesn't give you the right to come over here and badger me because your food is subpar." Nina fussed around with something and then handed him a dish of food. "This is real food!"

I wanted to cheer. Nina stood her ground against this bully. Before I could intervene, the man stomped his feet and stormed off, clutching the food. I watched until he rounded the block and was out of sight before I walked up to Nina's truck.

"Who was that?" I asked her.

"Connor. He operates a roach coach and usually

parks it over on the next block near the post office," Nina told me, her tone tight and irritated. "Every time we come here, he shows up and tries to scare us away with idle threats. We'll see how he feels after eating that," Nina smirked.

"Don't you think that was relevant information?" I asked, slamming my hands on my hips, not feeling bad for Connor. "Which truck is his?"

"Connor's Corner," Nina grumbled. "Everything he sells is deep-fried. There is not one fresh or handmade item on his menu. All frozen food he dips in the pancake batter then fries it. I didn't mention it to you because Connor is nothing but a pompous blowhard."

"I can tell. It's still important information to have, considering what we found this morning. Even pompous blowhards can be vindictive little pricks that become dangerous," I huffed out. "One of the local wolf pack is going to be watching over your property for the next couple of nights, so if you see a big wolf, please don't panic or try to hurt it. Also, as we talked about earlier, get security cameras set up. I contacted a witch to come out and place wards on your property as well, so be expecting her."

"Do you truly think all of that will be necessary?" Nina looked suddenly worried. "Can't I just feed them food that will make them do stupid things?"

"Yes, necessary," I insisted. "You have valuable skills, and small-minded people will feel threatened by that as you just witnessed."

"Fine," Nina agreed reluctantly. It was as if the roles were reversed from how I felt this morning eating the muffin.

Feeling somewhat vindicated, I instructed Nina and Ed to go straight home and be aware of their surroundings. I mean, when it comes down to it, they were both younger than my youngest son, so I was okay with bossing them around like a parent.

Now it was time for me to start digging into Connor of the roach coach. I thought about buying something to eat from him, however, if it were all fried, I'd get a case of heartburn, and that didn't sound too appealing to me. It sounded more like a food truck that catered to teenagers who didn't worry about the state of their health.

I wasn't sure if Connor was magical or not since I hadn't gotten close enough to sense anything. Yet, when I walked around the corner and saw a gigantic picture of Connor plastered on the side of his truck, I had to pause and wonder if he was deficient in the common-sense department.

If Nina hadn't told me the truck's name, I wouldn't have known it was a food truck. It was just Connor's picture and the words Connor's Corner. It wasn't a good picture either. Connor looked clown-like with a smile that someone painted on instead of a genuine one.

Indeed, just like I had expected, the only customers were a couple of teenage boys in sweats and beanies. These weren't the customers who would appreciate the food Nina and Ed made, and I was pretty sure that they would both be okay with not calling them lost customers.

Shrugging, I took a seat on a bench outside of a laundromat. I was trying to figure out how I could determine if Connor was magical or not. Finally settling on following him back to his house and snooping around, I relaxed, ready for a long day.

There were stretches of hours where no one approached the food truck, which didn't shock me in the least. It wasn't only the food; it was the man serving it that would deter me. More so than the promise of a greasy heartburn-filled night. However, the tool did eat Nina's food and became agitated, throwing plates out the

37

window at random and shouting curse words. Nina strikes back.

"You should have taken my offer of a job," a male voice said from my left.

I jolted hard and practically fell off the bench when my head swiveled to see who it was to find Wiley, the town's newest resident. A rich good looking one to boot and one embroiled in criminal activity that put others at risk. Mick and I had been searching for him to get proof of it all. What were the odds that he'd sit on the bench next to me?

I scoffed at his statement. "Why would I want to work for you?"

Wiley reached out and ran a finger down my arm, making my skin crawl like thousands of pissed-off fire ants were biting me. "We'd be good together, beautiful Risa."

"I'll let you dream about that, but if you ever touch me again, you won't like the consequences," I snarled, fury dripping from my voice.

"Do you think you can go head-to-head with me and come out the victor?" Wiley drawled. "You know nothing about me, my sweet. It's cute you think your small-town investigation services are up to the high bar of standards that I've set. I think Nina would make an excellent personal chef."

Wiley stood up, flicked his eyes over me with a gleam that I couldn't identify in them, and waltzed off towards Connor's food truck. I watched him, fuming and doing my best to control my instinct to charge after him and set my magic free.

My thoughts were racing, and instinctively, I pulled out my phone to call Danny. After a lot of rings, he finally answered.

"Hi, Risa," his voice came across the line, sad and sullen.

"Danny," I frowned at his tone. "Did you find out any useful information on Wiley?"

"Risa, we need to talk," Danny said, not answering my question. "I did something idiotic. I let myself get drunk, and uh, lost control of my responses. I slept with someone," he finally blurted out. "It wasn't my intent, and I was coerced into it. I'm so sorry."

I pulled the phone away from my ear and stared at it, no longer hearing the words that Danny rattled around. Something inside me snapped. I seriously liked Danny. My heart heavy, my temper on the verge of flaring out of control, I hung up the phone on him.

Chapter Seven

I still planned on following Connor. However, I knew I needed to let someone know what I had seen and had transpired with Wiley. If he was part of what was happening to Nina, things were dangerous on a level that said I needed backup.

I put my phone back to my head and listened as it rang. The masculine voice that answered made whatever snapped in me with Danny's phone call move to a different place. "What's wrong, Risa?" Mick growled.

I quickly told him about Wiley and what my plans were, saying nothing about Danny. Wiley was a problem that required the assistance of members of the town's council now that we've uncovered how deep his crimes have gone with the kidnapping and selling of species.

It didn't even touch on how I didn't know what he was or what his magic could do other than flip my Jeep and pursue me through the woods. Something about his magic smelled familiar to me, and if he was after Nina, then her skills must be highly sought after.

Mick grunted. "The council is divided on the subject of Wiley. If I'm right, some of them are already in his pocket or under his spell. He's gunning for you, Risa. Wiley has a target planted squarely on your back, and I want to know why. I've met some resistance on the topic of helping you.

It doesn't mean I won't, but it tells me that Wiley has been in their ears."

I didn't know what to say to that. I honestly had no idea why Wiley would be after me. "The only thing I did to that man was not accept work from him. I may have insulted his balls. Seriously, if he's that sensitive about his balls, he has bigger issues than me not taking his case."

Mick snorted, "Clearly. I've got two wolves assigned to watch Nina's place tonight and tomorrow night. I'll ask two more to keep an eye on Wiley's place. As for you, I'll find you and trail you."

Flustered, "I didn't mean I needed help. I only wanted someone to know what was going on. Nina is my concern."

"Too bad," Mick growled. "I know you are hiding something from me." Mick hung up, and once again, it left me staring at my phone.

That was why I was so set in my ways about relationships. Now that I was left alone with my thoughts again, I realized that Danny had been crying. I think I knew he wouldn't have chosen to cheat on me on some level, yet I didn't want to hear it. That information had hurt, and I couldn't process it at this moment.

I shoved the emotions down and decided to call Nina. "Hi, Nina, it's Risa," I choked out when she answered.

"What's wrong, honey?" Nina cooed.

"My boyfriend cheated on me," I blurted out and found myself digesting the words as I blinked slowly. "Uh, that's not why I called," I quickly tried to cover the truth faux pas. "Did your parents or anyone else in your line have special skills that you would have picked up on?"

"My father was a hell of a gardener," Nina thought out loud. "The women were all amazing cooks. You told me you think that's where I get the kitchen witch from, right?"

"Your father was a gardener?" I thought she had

42

told me that already, which probably meant he was a garden witch—mixed with kitchen witch that could be helpful. It also meant that someone could use Nina to grow herbs for an alchemist to make potions that could be deadly.

Stretching the imagination, sure, but it was Wiley I was considering. Given that Wiley had been actively hunting a purple people eater named Jonielle and that my oldest son, Gavin, was hired to create a potion that drained the magic from someone to bestow on someone else. The ingredients only existed on the property of a sasquatch that someone tried to run out of town; this kind of fit. It wouldn't surprise me in the slightest if Wiley were the mastermind behind it all in the larger picture of this.

"My dad was the best gardener I have ever seen. He's the one who taught me everything I know," Nina replied reverently. "We lost him not too long ago. I think of him every time I'm in the garden. Is that silly?"

"No," I answered honestly. "I think it's beautiful. Remember, there are going to be wolves watching over you the next couple of nights. If you can, stay in. I'm going to follow Connor. If he is a part of this, he's being used as a tool. I want to get the guy pulling the puppet strings."

"Okay," Nina agreed. "As for your boyfriend, I'm sorry. I'm going to make a batch of cookies for you. I've been reading my grandma's cookbook. I think I have the perfect recipe to use."

Danny wasn't an idiot, and I needed to remember that. We all made mistakes, and if the feeling of breaking inside me was any indication of how I felt about that man, I needed to examine things closer. For the moment, I was single again.

"Thank you, Nina. Oh, and if you get any job offers to be a personal chef, reject them. I believe there is something larger at play," I remembered to add.

43

"Oh, no worries there," Nina declared with a huff. "I have no interest in being someone's slave. I have kids and grandkids; they are demanding enough."

"I hear you there," I laughed, the emotions rolling through my guts, easing for a few seconds.

"Be safe tonight," Nina told me softly before hanging up.

I had no qualms that Wiley had outed me to Connor, given the way the slimy little man kept popping his head out of the food truck window to look at me. Not that it mattered, I was still going to follow him, even if he saw me. It would make him nervous, and people in that state of mind often made stupid mistakes, thinking they were more intelligent than the predator stalking them.

Connor started packing things in about an hour later. I got up from the bench and disappeared between the buildings to move closer to him without being seen while he was inside the truck. I maneuvered around the block to get a look at the license plate. I'd get his address from that; it was easy enough to get with a background check.

Once I snapped a picture with my phone, I made my way to my Jeep and startled myself with the reflection in my rearview mirror of my deep blue hair. The color was gorgeous, though I knew it meant I was depressed. I'd get over it. It wasn't the first time a man had hurt and disappointed me.

I reached for the hat sitting on my backseat and tucked my hair up inside the beanie to hide it from sight. There would be fewer questions that way. I drove back to my office to run the background search and refused to think about how much easier it would be to call and ask Danny to do it for me.

Nope, not going there. I ran into my office and searched, obtained Connor's address, and went back out to my Jeep. I needed some food to keep my energy levels up, so I stopped at a convenience store, loaded up on caffeine and chocolate, and got a few tacos for good measure. It was food, even if Gage would disagree.

Chapter Eight

My head was hot and itchy. I wanted to pull my beanie off and let air flow through my locks, but I sensed Mick was out there watching me. My mood hadn't changed enough for my hair to have turned back to blonde, and I didn't want to explain.

It was dark now, and I'd been watching Connor's house for the past three hours. The man wasn't smart. He kept moving the curtains to the side in the front window and peering out. It would have been more subtle to look through the peephole on his front door, not that he could see me.

Connor's eyesore of a truck blocked my Jeep from view, and I had also used a look-away charm that made people's eyes naturally not notice my red Jeep. Those little spells were handy in situations like this one. They didn't work on everyone, though they worked on most.

Two hours ago, I'd gotten confirmation that my witch contact had placed wards around Nina's property and her garden, and that gave me a slight sense of satisfaction. At least Nina would know her plants wouldn't be tampered with again.

I had myself convinced at this point that Connor was a pawn for Wiley. There was always a chance I was wrong, but it felt right to me. It still made Connor guilty of several crimes, and if I were lucky, someone would be able to worm out of him who put him up to the harmful shenanigans.

My Jeep rocked sideways suddenly, and I swallowed a scream at the giant wolf nose pressed to the window. Mick's canines looked exceptionally sharp with that weird wolfy smile thing he was doing. I knew he'd been out there, not because he said he would be trailing me, it was just the way my luck was going.

I got out of the Jeep. "What?" I whispered harshly. It was stupid of me since I didn't speak wolf and wouldn't be able to hear him telepathically like his pack.

I got it three seconds later when a non-descript car backed out of the driveway of Connor's house. I opened up my door, and Mick jumped in before I could get in, and I quickly followed, putting enough distance between us that Connor wouldn't notice me. I also had my headlights turned off through these dark streets.

It turns out that Connor was using the same type of charm I was using. It was hard to follow him, and only with Mick's interference was I able to stay on his trail. Mick would nip at my arm when I wanted to turn away from Connor.

"The little prick is a mage, isn't he?" I asked the wolf and got a huff back in response.

There was no doubt that Connor was heading for Nina's house. The houses and streets became familiar. Mages could be taught to channel their energy into magic, but they did need the inherent gene that identified them as magical. Witches were born into it and could tap into the earth's energy, making them more dangerous as that supply of power wasn't limited to what their body could hold.

Nina was at the top of her game with the natural skills she possessed, and I suspected that Connor was at the low end of the mage food chain. Look-away charms were easy to get. Regardless, this was going to be over tonight. I had the little pissant dead to rights caught in the act with an alpha wolf as a witness, along with whatever pack he had around Nina's.

Mick's paw shot out and hit the lever to shift my Jeep into neutral, and I got the hint that I needed to stop. We parked down the street from Nina's house, and I got out. Mick followed me, and we blended into the shadows and moved towards Connor.

He'd boldly parked right in front of Nina's house, trusting that look-away spell a little too much. We'd gotten close enough for me to hear him chanting in what sounded like Latin. I didn't speak Latin, but I knew enough to know the word *ignis* meant fire.

Connor was either trying to throw a fireball or set Nina's house on fire. I was two seconds too slow in my shout to make him stop. The spell, or charm, released a jet stream of fire at Nina's house as Connor whirled to see me standing there shouting at him.

A look of victory was splayed across his smarmy face as a mirror ward ignited behind him and sent the torrent of fire streaming directly back at him. Unfortunately for me, I was right behind him and in the path of the returning flames.

Connor let out an ear-piercing high-pitched little girl scream and fell face-first on the driveway as Mick's large wolf body slammed into me with the force of a freight train loaded with cannonballs. The air whooshed out of me in half a second flat, but not in time for the flames to miss us. My beanie ignited, and the tips of Mick's fur singed.

The menacing growl that emanated from the alpha was enough to slow me down and widen my eyes. The man wasn't happy. Mick's teeth nipped at my head, and he flung down the burning hat right before he rolled and smothered

49

the flames trying to burn his fur off his massive body.

Connor must have worn flame retardant clothing because that bastard was merely smoking instead of being a crispy mage. Howls pierced the air, and Nina appeared in the driveway, looking stunned.

I choked back a half-laugh, half-sob, as she marched right for Connor and let her foot fly, landing a perfect nut shot that doubled him over. To make it even more satisfying, she smashed the produce in her hands on his face. A hot pepper from the look of it, though Connor got no pity from me. He deserved it.

Mick shifted, which drew Nina's attention to the smoking, literally, hot naked man that took the place of the singed wolf. I didn't blame her one little iota for openly staring either. Her eyes shifted to me momentarily, and she started seeing the blue hair.

"We'll be discussing this color," Mick whispered in my ear before pulling on the sweats that another wolf appeared and dropped at his feet before blending back into the night. Mick stood over Connor, freezing him in place with a look while he called the Glimmering Rock police and reported the crime.

Nina sprouted a devious grin and ran inside, returning with a plate of cookies that she offered to Mick and then to me, citing her grandma's recipe. I was more than a little skeptical after seeing her grin, so I didn't bite into it as quickly as Mick did.

"Don't consider yourself safe now, Nina," I warned her. "Connor is a pawn for a larger player. Though, I do believe things will ease up for you."

Mick's heated stare distracted me from Nina for a moment when he stalked closer to me. "She's single," Nina called out to Mick.

Mick raised his eyebrow at me. "Is that so?" he rumbled in a deep husky tone.

50

"Uh, I'm on a case," I reminded the alpha wolf and pushed slowly to my feet. "Nina, that doesn't help," I told her around the bulky man in front of me. "Go back inside."

"Case closed!" Nina cheered. "You'll get your meals. Send me the invoice for your services *after* you take that man for a spin." Not helpful.

"It's not over, Mick," I lowered my voice. I had no clue if I was talking about my relationship with Danny or the case. "Wiley is still out there," I tried again.

Mick prowled closer after ordering Connor not to move and fingered my blue hair. "Did he hurt you?"

I didn't know who he was referring to, though I suspected it was about Danny. "Are the cops coming?" I tried to distract him.

"They are," Mick confirmed and took another bite of the cookie, which made his eyes darken with lust.

Well, damn. Nina was a tricky little witch. Lust cookies. I devoured my cookie, curious to see how this would play out. Life as a private investigator wasn't always dull.

Book 7
Pooka-Boo

Chapter One

My name is Risa Sanders. You all know that. I'm the owner and sole investigator of I S.P.I, a supernatural and paranormal investigative firm here in town. But, of course, you all know that as well," I haughtily addressed the town council, going through their stupid formality.

"Glimmering Rock has suddenly sprouted several unusual cases that I feel may be connected, with the town's new resident as the puppet master behind it all," I continued, pacing a little. "I feel the remaining residents could be at risk, and you should do something to assist the effort to prove the crimes."

"Are you suggesting we assign police to this ridiculous idea that you are falsely accusing an innocent man of crimes there is no proof he committed?" Councilmember Vern sneered at me.

"What is the harm in listening to her?" Councilmember Penelope asked.

I wasn't sure I could trust Penelope Pine, but she was dating my sasquatch friend, Ax, so I'd give her the benefit of the doubt. "Thank you, councilwoman Pine," I responded respectfully. "I have been pursued by Wiley through the woods while trying to rescue a purple people eater and return her to her realm where she wouldn't be starving. Before you ask, I know that it was Wiley due to the magical signature."

"Your magic isn't trustworthy; it's never worked," Vern snapped. "It's well documented."

Mick, the wolf pack's alpha and a council member, shifted in his seat and frowned at Vern. I knew Mick wasn't against me, though he was often difficult for me to read. "Risa isn't lying, as I was there in that instance and can verify her claim."

The closed-door session of the council meeting was trying every last bit of my patience. It had taken me two weeks even to get the opportunity to address the council, and I am positive that Mick had a part in making it happen. His motives I couldn't be sure of, but that was a different issue.

"The town is in danger," I insisted, putting every bit of confidence I had in me into the statement.

"It's been said that you are the danger to this town," Temperance, a djinn, stated with no inflection to her tone.

There wasn't one person sitting behind that blasted table that didn't suddenly blink and shift, their wide eyes glued to me. Mick moved and touched his hair subtly, a sign that my hair had just changed color, and I could guess without looking that it was bright red since I was angry.

I glanced at Mick again and saw the slight shake of his head. Huffing out an irritated sigh, I rolled my eyes. "You all need help. Regardless of the history of my magic, I know danger when it presents itself. If you all want to be fooled by the promise of funding or power, whichever it is he's offering, then it's on your head if shit hits the fan."

I turned and strode with my back straight right from the room, slamming the doors behind me. Childish? Possibly, but I didn't care at this point. I should have known that they wouldn't hear me out. Mick had warned me that they were questioning me; nothing new with that either. I had a reputation with the lawmakers and law enforcers, both here in Glimmering Rock, the magical town, and Branstone, the non-magical city that hid Glimmering Rock.

Whatever, I had a one hundred percent success rate—the cops couldn't say that. I practically stomped my way out of the building into the night. Meetings got held at night due to Vern being a vampire.

I halted suddenly, my feet sticking to the ground as if someone had dropped me in quicksand. Danny stood at the tail of my red Jeep. Two weeks ago, he told me he'd slept with someone else. I wasn't ready to deal with that yet.

Steeling my heart, I resolved to get into my Jeep without breaking down or causing a scene of some sort. Honestly, with my newly blooming magic, anything was possible. If my magic reacted, it would only reinforce the instilled belief that I was the danger in this town. Where the hell was my leprechaun magic when I needed it?

No sooner than that thought had passed through my mind, I spotted a slender woman trotting up to me. "Risa Sanders?" the woman asked.

"Yeah, that's me," I answered. I held my hand up to the woman for a moment and turned my attention back to Danny. "You'd be wise not to speak to me."

A pressing feeling of needing to kneel and submit washed over me, and I sighed heavily. The woman who had approached me dropped to her knees and bent her head in supplication. No way was I doing that. The only benefit to the display of power was Danny shuffled off, not wanting to deal with Mick any more than I did—only for very different reasons.

I glanced over my shoulder at the alpha wolf and rolled my eyes again. "Thanks," I said grudgingly. It wouldn't be much longer that he would wait for an explanation about what happened between Danny and me.

I didn't think it was his business, but Mick seemed to think otherwise.

Mick gave me a terse nod and went back into the building and the suffocating feel of the alpha command released. The woman got to her feet and shook herself. She held her hand out to me, "Hi, Risa. I'm Tina."

I shook her hand and led us over to a picnic table in the greenbelt next to the town hall. "Hi, Tina. What can I do for you?"

"Word of mouth brings me to you. I hear you have a great success rate with your cases, and I think I require a private investigator. I don't have proof to bring to the police to press charges against anyone, and I don't know who is behind everything. I think someone is trying to scare me out of my house," Tina explained after we sat.

Eerily similar to the case that Ax had brought to me a couple of months ago. "Why do you think that?" I asked her. "Do you have flying dogs?"

Tina gave me an odd look and shook her head. "No. I have horses and one dog, but she doesn't fly. Can I ask what that alpha thing was?"

Sure, Tina could ask all she wanted, it didn't mean I was going to tell her. "Ignore it. Men think with their dicks. Tell me what's going on, or if you'd rather, you can meet me at my office tomorrow morning."

"Now works for me. My grandma and I are currently at the hotel in town. Night seems to be when the activity at the house is the strongest, and she needs some sleep," Tina shrugged. "We live on the coast."

I could use the distraction. "Okay, let me have it."

Chapter Two

My grandma and I live on a tract of property on the coast. I have horses that I board, train, and my own. My grandma gardens and does her own thing for the most part, but since she's up there in age, I watch over her. Earlier this year, a couple of people stopped by asking about the property and if we were interested in selling it. My grandma, Deloris, is a bit of a smart ass at times and replied that for the right price, anything is for sale," Tina told me.

"I'm guessing they took that to heart?" I quirked my lips in amusement and leaned against the table with my elbow.

"Bingo. They began calling all the time, sending letters, and making offers," Tina said with an irritated tone. "We aren't selling. I threatened to press harassment charges against them, and two weeks later, the weirdness began."

"What does weirdness mean to you?" I had to ask because what I thought was weird varied considerably from other people.

"Understand," Tina went on, "we've lived there a long time with nothing happening. I think we'd have noticed an influx of ghosts before now, and that's what happened. Then we got bogus stories in the mail about mass murders happening on the property. It's total bullshit."

"Was it just ghost stories, or are there actual ghosts there?" I was intrigued.

"Actual ghosts, and those jerks are loud! My poor grandma can't get any sleep!" Tina thumped her fist on the table angrily. "She's an old woman. Where's the respect?"

I snorted because it seemed like respect had gone down the toilet a while ago. "Can you both see ghosts?"

"Yep, we sure can! We are pookas," Tina declared proudly. "Here's the kicker; I think the ghosts were hired. They aren't even specter's wandering around lost, unable to move on. They are just pests."

"What the hell does a ghost pimping themselves out like that do for them? You can't pay them!" I burst out, caught up in Tina's frustration. I smiled a foolish grin. "I guess that's what you need me to find out, right?"

"That, and who is behind it, and how do we get rid of the damn ghosts?" Tina thumped the table again. "I can't shoot them like I do rats."

Pookas were apparently very temperamental. Who knew? "Why did you bow to Mick?" I veered off subject for a moment.

"Did you not feel that power?" Tina asked incredulously. "He's a shifter alpha. He might not be my alpha, but I knelt out of respect."

I needed to brush up on my pooka knowledge. "I thought you were fae," I admitted.

"We are, but we are also a shifter. Iron will hurt us," Tina informed me.

"Aren't horseshoes iron?" I blurted out stupidly.

"Steel," Tina replied. "Iron is a component of it, and I wear gloves if I have to shoe a horse."

I needed to shut up before Tina decided I was way too much of an idiot to be hired to help her and her grandmother. "Do you have an email address? I can email the contract for you to look over and sign."

"Oh, I sure do!" Tina grinned and slid a card across the table to me. *Horsin' Around* was written across the top. "Does that mean you'll take the case?"

"Yeah, I'll take it. Is this your house address?" I asked, tapping the card.

"Yes. I look forward to the contract. I'll get it signed and back to you right away," Tina promised. She reached out, shook my hand, and then pranced off. Tina moved like a horse, now that I thought about it. Strong and graceful.

Pocketing the card, I stood up and made my way to the Jeep before Mick came back out and cornered me into talking about my new single status. In my last case, a kitchen witch named Nina made lust cookies that almost had me mounting the alpha in her driveway after she fed them to us while waiting for the police to arrive.

Moving quickly, I headed home and hoped the philandering Danny wasn't there waiting for me. I had pooka research to do, a contract to send, and maybe a bottle of wine to drink. Though I couldn't lie to myself, the thought of taking Mick for a spin kept surfacing, even if I knew it was a bad idea.

Chapter Three

Pookas, or púcaí if I wanted to use the correct spelling, which I didn't, were known to be a bit devious. They could be either helpful or not so friendly. That about summed up everyone. I found frequent references to them being mischievous, and that didn't surprise me at all. Pooka was of the fairy family, and could shift into horses, cats, hares, dogs, and goats.

Tina moved like a horse, so it made sense to me that when she shifted, that is what she chose. A fae horse was pretty badass, in my opinion. I pulled out the card Tina had given me and sent over my standard contract via email.

I took the initiative to plug Tina's address into the search engine to see if I found any legitimate stories about things happening there. I couldn't find anything that would warrant the activity Tina mentioned, but I did note that the property had beach access. I imagine there are plenty of people that would find that desirable—me included.

Standing up and pacing around behind my desk, I decided to imagine why Wiley wanted that property. I didn't know that it was him behind it, but since he kept surfacing, blaming him felt good. Wiley was wealthy, new to town, arrogant, evil in my estimation, and known to be part of a trafficking operation. So why wouldn't he be the force behind running Tina out of her home?

It was wrong of me to assume that Wiley was at the root of Tina's problem, and my conscience should have prickled at me for jumping to conclusions—it didn't.

I glanced at my watch, eleven o'clock. I knew that Tina and her grandmother were at the hotel in town, which meant the property was uninhabited, giving me the perfect opportunity to go out there and see what was happening. Technically, I would be trespassing since I didn't have a signed contract back from Tina yet, though she did say most of the activity was happening at night.

Like a magical charm, my email dinged with perfect timing, showing me a signed contract from Tina. The legal issue was moot now. Thank you, leprechaun blood.

I darted to the kitchen where I had dropped my keys, snatched them up, and wasted no time in flinging open my door and plowing face-first into a solid wall of chest muscle. Oh damn. The smell of Mick washed over my senses in a millisecond, and instead of removing my face from between two well-defined pecs, I inhaled him.

Mick's low-pitched growl reverberated through my ears. His arms wrapped loosely around my back. "Why is your hair half red and half lavender? What are you feeling?"

"Lust and passion," I answered automatically. *Idiot,* I berated myself silently. I reluctantly pushed away from the infuriating wolf. "Didn't mean to crash into you, sorry about that. I'm on my way out."

"Where are you going?" Mick narrowed his eyes and kept his arms around my back while allowing me to inch away from his chest. Then, without allowing me to answer, he dipped his head and sniffed my neck. "Shit, you aren't lying about the lust. What happened with Daniel?"

Startled at the use of Danny's proper name and the sniff test, I blinked in response. "I've got to go. I've got a case I'm working on."

Mick's arms dropped away, and the cool evening air

did nothing to calm the heat racing through me. His eyes were calculating as they probed my face for answers I wasn't voicing. The man was intense, and I had the irrational urge to do something to make him as flustered as he made me.

Stepping to the side of him, his eyes still on mine, I slid my hand out and cupped his junk. It didn't escape my notice that it was hard either. His eyes flashed yellow for a brief second, the only indication that I ruffled him. "Hope they aren't too blue," I quipped as I bolted for my Jeep.

The sound of deep laughter reached my ears as I hopped in and quickly locked the door. Like something as insignificant as a locked vehicle door would stop that wolf shifter. I resisted the urge to peel out of my driveway and drove as calmly as my jittery nerves would allow. Touching Mick as I had was playing with fire.

Chapter Four

It was a sad state of affairs that the palm of my hand burned with the memory of the feel of Mick. My mind filled the entire drive out to Tina's with thoughts of what I'd like to do with the man instead of focusing on driving. I needed to bite the bullet and talk with Danny, or alternately, take Mick for a joyride.

I pulled down the drive to Tina's with no conscious thought of having driven here. The first thing I saw was the horse barns and fields where they roamed, though the fields were devoid of life from what I could see. Next, my headlights illuminated another area fenced in, where I assumed Tina did some training with the animals.

Beyond that was a clearing with what appeared to be chicken wire fencing and poles. It had to be the garden that Tina's grandma Deloris worked in. The area seemed significant, and I shook my head in admiration that someone had the patience and skill to make something grow like that. It briefly reminded me of Nina's lush garden.

Past the garden, closer to the cliff, was the rustic-looking house. One-level ranch-style with a covered porch and lots of windows. Behind the house was a thick forest. The setting offered the best of both worlds: a high perch with woods close enough to the beach to provide the sea air, the sound of the waves, and a path leading down to the water.

I parked the Jeep and got out, breathing the scent of the saltwater and pine trees deeply. I would not sell this place, and it angered me that someone was trying to run them out of their home. I walked towards the house a few steps and smiled at the old rusty water pump with an old tin bucket perched under it.

The closer to the house, I let my senses get all heightened, watching for signs of activity. A few more strides towards the porch revealed a rocking chair holding sentry, looking foreboding and inviting at the same time due to the dark shadows dancing across the front of the house.

A horse neighed, sounding much closer than it was, making me jump a little. I frowned at my edginess and blamed the council for my unsettled nerves. I wanted to think Mick was at fault, but then I'd have to admit my part in that, and I was prideful enough to avoid that thought.

I was, at most, three steps away from the stair to the porch when a tingle went over my spine that told me I wasn't alone. A half a second later, that little tin bucket I found so charming smacked me in the back with a painful thump. I wasn't amused.

Spinning my body around, I let my gaze rove across the landscape, looking for movement. After the third scan, a small orb of light caught my eye. I took a step towards where it disappeared, and a twinge in my back kept me still for a heartbeat. I sucked in a breath and grit my teeth, bending over to pick up the bucket and forced myself to move to the pump, where I placed the offending item back in its place.

Righting myself, I ignored the throbbing place on my spine and turned back to the house. "Show yourself, coward." I knew my tone wasn't friendly—I wasn't in that frame of mind, thanks to the bucket to the back.

Tina hadn't mentioned violence, and the thought of a grandma getting subjected to that enraged me. So I stalked back to the porch with no hesitation this time and turned to plop my ass on the stair, dangling my hands between my knees.

"I'm not afraid of you, asshole. Show yourself." My voice didn't travel far, telling me there was something in front of me absorbing the sound. I saw the projectile this time and swatted the rock out of the air. "Surprise. I'm not an old lady that's bothered by the antics."

The rocking chair behind me moved, and I didn't turn. I didn't even flinch, even though my heart stuttered a few beats. Given the areas of activity, Tina had been right; there was more than one ghost here. My skin was pricking with the awareness of being watched by several somethings.

The creaking of the rocking chair became joined by the handle of the rusty pump moving and what sounded like a chorus of tap dancers performing on gravel. I slowly shook my head at the childish attempt to scare me.

"Is that all you've got?" I challenged them. Not my brightest move, to be sure, though my goading was to provoke the spirits to materialize. I needed to get answers on why they were here. It might be a tad hard since I typically couldn't understand ghosts; I could only see them. It called for some creative thinking on my part.

The bucket launched at me again, this time with more force. It irked me that the damn ghosts were working together because while I was preparing for the bucket to hit, the rocking chair hurtled unseen towards my head.

The crack of the wood on my skull made me see stars, and my ears buzz. I barely had time to block the bucket with my arms when my legs got forcibly yanked, tumbling me back on the steps. That was when I noticed there was a hanging flower basket above me. Only it wasn't hanging—it was descending on my face. The impact hurt like hell, and I blacked out.

Chapter Five

My eyes cracked open to the sound of angry honking geese and the smell of flatulence. Groaning, I pushed myself to sit upright, felt weight sitting on my feet, and I realized that Mick was there. "Are you farting?" I resisted the urge to pinch my throbbing nose.

The baleful look the wolf gave me almost made me laugh. I blinked the fog away from my eyes and tried to focus. It didn't surprise me Mick was here—so were the ghosts. I saw at least twenty of them surrounding us, all of them making noise.

"Ghosts with gas, great. My night has reached its peak of fun." I gingerly felt the back of my head for knots and moved my hands around to under my nose. Sticky blood coated my fingers. "It's broke, isn't it?" I asked the wolf.

I didn't need Mick to nod his big head at me. I could feel the pain. "Help me up." I reached my hands out and gripped his thick fur, which is all I needed to do since he was so large. All Mick had to do was stand up, and it lifted me to my feet. I patted his head. "Thanks, pup."

Mick nipped my fingers at my remark and hovered around me while I took in the scene. These ghosts were scraping the bottom of the barrel of the spirit realm from what I could see. They looked like failed clowns trying to be zombies.

"Can you see these jokers?" I nudged the wolf with my hip. "Talk about a spiritual fiasco. Even if Tina had told me what to expect, I don't think I would have understood."

I don't know why I was still intentionally trying to rile them up. The ghosts had already proven they could take me down. Mick huffed, and I was pretty sure he couldn't see ghosts, which was a shame because it would have been good for a laugh.

"Alright, assholes. Enough with the assault. Keep it up, and I'll bring back someone that can banish you to a hellish afterlife and ensure you'll never see anything in this realm ever again," I threatened. "Honestly, I should do that anyway."

A few of the ghosts shimmered for a moment and then popped out of sight. Mick let out an impatient wolf sigh, followed by a hair-raising menacing growl that had me stepping away from him. I wasn't sure what he was reacting to, and I narrowed my eyes, trying to look mean.

One of the more rotund ghosts stepped forward. The ghoul was wearing a wife-beater shirt full of holes that didn't stretch over his expansive belly or meet the waistband of the dirty sweats he was sporting like a pro. The double chin had a chin, and the thin lips did nothing to hide the missing teeth. Beady eyes glared at me from under a bald dome with a ring of curls over his ears. All that was missing was the painted-on clown smile.

The ghost's mouth opened, and again I heard the honking geese. It made me snicker a bit while maintaining the creepy factor. The offensive smell permeated the air around us, causing the alpha wolf shifter to sneeze and move positions. Sad when I could smell it through a bloody and broken nose.

"I can't understand you." I waved my hand in front

of my face trying to fan the noxious air away. "Whoever sent you here, give it up. Leave. Tina and Deloris don't want you here, and I don't blame them. However, you have no claim on this land, and I'm prepared to take measures to remove you permanently."

Another growl erupted from Mick, causing me to step away again, and promptly tripped over something, dumping me on my ass. Mick moved fast, his tail whipping me in the face as he turned, making my eyes instantly tear as the pain registered. I didn't see the objects hurled at us due to that. I only tasted fur as Mick threw his large wolf body at me.

"Good heavens!" Tina's voice reached me through the ruckus of honking geese, objects raining down on us, and rocks clinking on that damn tin bucket.

Fear for her safety activated the magic inside of me that allowed me to get my ass kicked by ghosts, and a dome-type shield sparked out of my fingertips. That single burst of magic was enough to shock the spirits into ceasing their assault. Gaping vapor mouths hung open, exposing rotting tongues and blackened teeth. Gross.

"Tina! What are you doing here?" I shoved against Mick, trying to get him to move.

"The cameras on the property alerted me that someone was here, and I came to investigate." Tina looked around and snarled at the round man who still hung around. "He's the worst of the bunch."

"Worst looking," I snorted. "Sorry, I should have told you I was going to look around. I was feeling restless, and once you sent back the contract, I figured I'd come to look since you said the activity was bad at night." I shakily got to my feet and steadied myself against Mick when my head swam.

"Grandma insisted I come take a look. She didn't want deer in her garden." Tina shrugged and examined my face. "Good grief, you are looking a little rough, and that's a hell of a dog you've got there."

It hurt my face, but I giggled. "That dog is the same one you bowed to earlier."

Chapter Six

Mick hadn't shifted back yet, but the wolf's eyes remained on me, and I couldn't decipher the look. I'm confident whatever he was trying to convey, it wasn't good. After all, he'd been called pup and dog and gotten beaned with objects by ghosts he couldn't see.

"Why didn't you tell me that these cockwaffles were physical?" I questioned Tina as we righted the overturned furniture.

"They never have been before. Not with us anyway, only with making things move." Tina glanced up at me with a worried expression. "Do you think they will harm my grandma?"

I shrugged; I didn't know how to answer that. "I did provoke the bastards, but only after one of them threw the bucket at me. Otherwise, I was only here to check things out."

Mick moved and stuffed his nose into my crotch, growling softly. Tina laughed when I tried to push him away. "Go home, asshole," I flicked his ear and whispered the words. All he did was move away, shift, and sit his naked junk in my Jeep.

"I'm going to bring my grandma to your office tomorrow before I bring her back here. Maybe between us, we can strategize on how to make sure I can keep her safe," Tina decided, chuckling as I watched the infuriating man.

"That's fine," I agreed. "Have your cameras picked up any people hanging around?"

"Not since these bastards showed up. Before that, a woman wandered back here saying she was lost and gave me some bogus address she was looking for; my grandma shifted into a very scary version of a pooka horse. Imagine a demon horse. Grandma Deloris hasn't shifted for a while, and doing so took a lot out of her, but I have to say, the reaction was priceless." Tina let out a snort of laughter at the memory.

I glanced over to where the naked wolf shifter sat in my Jeep and found those unreadable eyes locked on me again. Refocusing my gaze on Tina, I asked, "Scary version? I didn't know there were different versions you could change into."

"Oh, sure. We can change into anything, really. Grandma Deloris used a horse since this was during the daytime, and I had horses out and was training. Only this woman didn't expect a nightmare hellish looking horse to come charging at her," Tina explained with an amused expression. "I've done it a couple of times myself to get rid of the religious people that show up and try to convert you."

At that visual, I did laugh and then stopped when the pain hit. "Epic. I would have loved to see that. Alright, we'll meet in my office. I won't be in before ten, but anytime after will be okay."

Tina nodded her acceptance and walked me halfway to my Jeep. "I'm going to respect his privacy and not look, even though I want to."

"I gotta say, it's worth it." I wasn't going to lie, and I wasn't going to force her to look either. I wanted the view all to myself.

"See you in the morning," Tina waved to me as I opened my Jeep door and saw the mouthwatering view presented to me.

Mick smirked at me as I looked my fill. "Tastes good, too. I'll share." The wink was what dampened the fires in my pants.

"Nah. I'm not a fan of marshmallows, and how would you know how it tastes? Oh wait, I know, dogs lick their own balls." I buckled my seatbelt and headed back home. "Can you send Crowley to me if you see him before I do?" Crowley was a medium and a seer that frequented Mick's bar.

Mick chuckled at my brush-off but agreed. "You need your nose looked at, Risa. Wouldn't hurt to have your back checked out, either. You took some hard hits."

"Why do you care? Why do you keep rescuing me? Seems extreme only to get laid." I got the nerve to spit out the words and waited with a suspended breath.

"Fuck if I know," Mick sighed. "You've got a mouth like a viper, insults for days, draw danger like a magnet, and put me in precarious situations too often. Yet you watched me come inside some bar rat with a cool indifference that has my wolf demanding I make you scream my name. He hates seeing you hurt, he likes the taste and smell of you, and I can't argue with that." He paused to glance at me. "Also, that ass makes me want to beg."

I had nothing to say to any of that. "You don't like me, but your wolf does?" I guess I had something to say after all.

Mick let a belly laugh fly. "That's not what I said. I like you well enough, Risa. One kiss after a spelled cookie wasn't quite sufficient to satisfy the hunger you incite in me. However, I'm not a poacher. What happened between you and Daniel? You aren't acting like a jilted woman, which tells me it's something petty."

77

This time it was me who laughed. A bitter and hurt laugh that I knew Mick heard all the intonations I didn't want him to. I said nothing and drove silently. Mick let out a quiet curse and planted his fist in the dashboard, leaving a dent that wouldn't be easy to fix.

"Shit. I'll fix that," Mick promised. "I'm sorry, Risa. So he fucked someone else and expects you to accept that?" His voice filled with righteous anger on my behalf. "I should have let my wolf have control earlier."

I pulled into the parking lot of Mick's bar and said nothing. My face throbbed; I was tired and now seriously confused. Mick made me feel wanted and like prey at the same time. I didn't know what to do with that.

Chapter Seven

My youngest son Jameson was waiting for me at home, telling me Mick somehow got ahold of him and told Jameson I needed some healing. I was in too much pain to read him a riot act, so I quietly accepted the offered help and then went to bed.

Waking up gave me a fresh perspective, one where I looked like I'd spent hours in a boxing ring with my face as the bag. Fantastic. Maybe I could walk around with a sack over my head. It would probably call less attention to myself.

I got ready to head to my office, didn't bother with makeup, and grabbed my travel coffee mug. That was the essential item of the day. I pulled a hat down over my head to shield my face, and out the door I went, with a glance at my watch. I'd get to my office right at ten if there were no traffic.

Luck was on my side, and I made it with two minutes to spare. So did Tina. I let out a dramatic sigh at the sight of Crowley. *No rest for the wicked,* I told myself. I almost expected Mick to materialize to round out the circus. I couldn't explain the letdown feeling when the wolf didn't surface.

"Good morning, ladies," I cheerfully called out as I slid out of my Jeep. "Thanks for coming, Crowley. I'll get the office unlocked."

I rushed inside to the locked door and hoped like mad that I hadn't left the office a mess because I had no time to get it cleaned up. As I shoved the key in the lock, I ripped the envelope taped to my door off and flung the door open, taking a quick look around. It was decent.

Three seconds behind me was Tina's grandma, Deloris; I assumed that's who she was since she marched right past me and into the office and looked back at me expectantly. Crowley followed her in and let out a quiet exclamation at what I didn't know, and I didn't have time to ask because then Tina walked in. I let the door close behind her and went to toss my keys on my desk.

Crowley was staring as if there was a carcass on display, and Deloris suddenly shifted into what I loosely have to describe as the scary pooka. It startled me so badly that I fell back into the devil chair, which promptly responded by launching me at the ceiling. I had a half of a millisecond to throw my arms up to block my face and hope the landing didn't hurt.

It felt like the ceiling pushed back on impact, and the rapid descent would have been a lot more amusing if it wasn't for my battered body that would be leaving the Risa-shaped dent in the floor. Yet, surprisingly soft and strong arms wrapped around me, saving me from my embarrassing fate.

"Goodness, dear," Crowley set me on my feet. "That was certainly memorable. What in Hades happened to your face? And did you know there is an entity in that chair? That pooka scared the bee-jaysus out of it."

Words wouldn't form. I looked back at Deloris, and she was once again her, not whatever nightmare creature she had shifted into for a moment. Feeling flustered, I sat on the edge of my desk and realized I still had an envelope clutched in my hand. I looked at it and, throwing caution to

80

the wind, ripped it open to have a condom fall out and land on my lap.

Get used to the idea. It's going to happen. Mick.

I felt the blush rising and bless Crowley; he plucked the condom from my lap, the note from my hand, and shoved both in a desk drawer. I found myself speechless for the second time this morning.

"Hello, I'm Crowley." I watched as he held his hand out to Deloris.

"Deloris." She shook his hand and returned to glaring at the offending desk chair. I understood that look on a cellular level.

"Tina," she offered her hand to Crowley. "We've hired Risa to help us at our house."

"I'm gonna go out on a limb and assume that's why she asked me here," Crowley moved and patted me gingerly on the back. "She's a good girl."

That snapped me out of my stupor. I cleared my throat. "Yes, Crowley is in a unique position to help me. But, with that said, Crowley, this might carry risk with it.' I gestured to my face. "The ghosts at their house are not nice ones."

I gave a brief rundown of my experience last night and saw Deloris narrow her eyes. "You should have them sit in that chair," Deloris smarted off. "It will devour their ridiculous dead souls. If those fools messed with my garden or my roses, there is going to be hell to pay."

"It was just me that got messed with." I did my best to reassure the woman. "Crowley is a medium, and I hope that he can tell me what they are saying. I can see them, but all I hear is honking geese. I plan to come back to your house this evening at dusk. There might be a chance Crowley can move them on, or at the very least, figure out why they are there."

"Ah, yes," Crowley agreed. He glanced at Tina. "Do

81

you have one of those in you?" Crowley's eyes shifted to Deloris.

Tina laughed, "I do."

"Rightfully terrifying. Maybe you two should bring those out and scare the ghosts." Crowley smiled to try and show he was joking; only I didn't think he was. "I'm fine with the risk, Risa. However, I do have to warn you that I was commanded to call the alpha if it looked like things were getting out of hand for you."

"Don't worry about that," I scowled at Crowley. "Tina, is it okay with you if we show up around dusk? I'll probably have a bit of equipment with me if I can get my hands on it. Those things that you see on TV that the people use who are trying to find ghosts."

"Absolutely," Tina answered quickly. "Grandma will stay inside, right Grandma?" Tina shot a take no prisoners look at her grandma.

"I'll do exactly as I see fit," Deloris leveled her own look at Tina.

"We are only trying to keep you safe, ma'am," I tried, using my best placating voice.

"Seems to me you'd be better off trying to keep yourself safe, or have you not looked in a mirror?" Deloris retorted smartly. "It looks like that fat slob of a ghost stepped on your face. That hat doesn't hide jack, missy."

Chapter Eight

I stared a hole through the salesman trying to sell me an electromagnetic field reader. "As I've said, I can already see ghosts. I can't understand them. Why do I need equipment that will tell me a ghost is present if I can use my eyeballs to tell me the same thing? I only need the recorder."

Crowley, next to me, snickered. "It's a last resort, as I can understand them."

We were in Branstone, and the salesman looked at us like we were insane. I couldn't have cared less. "Please, that is all we need. Ring it up. We have ghosts to go chase."

It was only in places like this that I could get away with saying things like that in the non-magical city. It felt good too. Even with the crazy look that the clerk gave me when I said I could see them. Time was wasting, and I did my best to control my irritation when the man finally decided we weren't going to buy anything else and rang us up.

Crowley grabbed the bag and followed me out of the store. "You need to eat something before we go out there. Mick was adamant that I take care of you, and I'll be damned if I'm going to piss that man off purposely."

"Relax, I'm going to go into that deli and get us some sandwiches to take with us; Mick can kiss my ass. It's not his job, or yours, to take care of me. It's my job, and I've managed to do that just fine for the last three hundred years. So it's not like he will be surprised if you tell him I didn't listen to you."

Crowley chuckled lightly. "Kissing your ass is something he would gladly do."

I was not going to have this conversation with Crowley. I crossed the street and walked into the deli to read the menu. I glanced at the monstrous sandwich that was handed to the customer at the counter and smiled. I'd get my money's worth here. "What do you like?" I asked Crowley.

"All of it," Crowley grinned at me and rubbed his belly. No sooner than he did that when his eyes went out of focus, and he began to sway.

Shit. It wasn't a good time for Crowley to have a vision, not in a crowded deli in Branstone. But, unfortunately, I couldn't snap him out of it either. So instead, I gently led him to an unoccupied table and sat him down, facing the wall.

"Is he okay, miss?" an employee asked me.

"Yes. Low blood sugar and not enough sleep," I smiled, thinking quickly.

I left him there and took my place in line to order us food. Once I got the food and drinks, I grabbed a handful of napkins, stuffed them in the bag, and went to collect Crowley. Thankfully, the vision was over, but he looked shaken.

"Bad one?" I asked gently, helping him stand, then handed him a drink. He gratefully took large gulps of the sugary liquid before nodding at me. "Does it have to do with the case tonight?" Crowley shook his head in response. I let out a small sigh of relief.

"Maggie," Crowley finally spoke, his voice trembling.

Maggie was a young female wolf shifter from Mick's pack that had gone missing almost a month ago. I was afraid to ask about the vision, but since Mick had hired me to help on that case as well, I knew I would need to hear the information before long.

"Is she alive?" I hesitated before asking the question we all wondered.

"She is," Crowley confirmed and said nothing else.

"I'll need to know the rest of it, but if you can't talk about it just yet, that's fine too." I patted Crowley's arm as we walked back to the Jeep.

"She's being held captive," Crowley whispered. "I can't see where, but it's dark, and she's injured. I don't think she's bathed; her hair is stringy, and she doesn't look healthy. I smelled sickness."

I got the sense that he wasn't telling me something, and I understood that he didn't want to talk about it yet. So I let it lie with what he said and filed the information away to speak with Mick about later. To Crowley's credit, talking about Maggie while we were in Branstone was a bad idea anyway.

We got in the Jeep and headed to Tina's. I mentally tried to prepare myself for more ghostly assaults. *Okay, magic,* I spoke to the center of my soul. *Don't let me down this time. We need to keep everyone safe.* I didn't even get a tingle back that my magic understood I needed it to be ready and responsive. How long was this puberty stage going to last?

"Danny knew what he was doing, though he thought it was you," Crowley added in a soft voice.

Great. Like I needed to be thinking about that right now. "Not talking about that, Crowley."

"Forgive, but never forget. I'm only saying there is

85

more to the story. However, Danny was aware of what he was doing," Crowley continued as if I hadn't spoken.

"Right." I wasn't sure I wanted to know the rest of the story.

Chapter Nine

I parked the Jeep in the same place I had parked last night and hopped out of the Jeep. Deloris was in the garden, and Tina was lying in the grass with a rifle propped against her shoulder like she was a soldier in war and creeping up on the enemy. *Crack!* The rifle fired.

Tina chambered another round and let off another shot before she raised her head from the sights and grinned in our direction. "Two more down. I wish I could shoot the ghosts that easily."

A couple of horses pranced around in the field nervously, spooked by the gunfire or by our presence; I wasn't sure. "I brought sandwiches for us all." I held up the bag and shook it lightly.

"That was nice of you! Grandma! Come out of the garden and eat with us," Tina called to Deloris. She pointed to a brown horse with a white splotch on his nose. "That's Zahbaar. I've had him since he was a babe." The horse nickered in response. "I'll put him in the barn before things get crazy tonight. Z is a sensitive soul."

"Come on. Let's have it. Bring the food out before you lock the old lady in the house," Deloris muttered as she walked up to us.

I had to hand it to her; the old girl had spunk. I hoped I was like her when I got older. I mean older than three hundred and change. You know, the seven hundred range or something like that. Who am I kidding? I'm going to be the woman everyone is afraid of because they won't be able to predict what will come out of my trashy mouth.

Tina led us to a table and chairs out on the porch, and I took the food out and laid it out. "Pick what you want; I'll take whatever is left."

"How magnanimous of you," Deloris quipped, grabbing a sandwich. "I bet the lettuce isn't as good as the quality in my garden."

I couldn't help it; I laughed. "I want to be like you when I grow up." Deloris winked at me and dove into her sandwich.

"Crusty old woman," Tina grinned and picked a sandwich after Crowley took his. "That's why we love her so."

Crowley was oddly silent, and I didn't push him to be social. I could feel the spirits around us, even if they weren't antagonizing us yet. I knew he had to be paying attention to them on some level. He only sat there and ate his food, his eyes roaming around the land.

Tina propped her rifle against the house and dug in. "Do you mind if I hang around while you are out here tonight?"

"Of course not," I told her. I slowly unwrapped my sandwich and took a bite, taking my time. Jameson might have healed me, but my facial movements were still tender as the bruises still existed.

"Is your friend going to show up?" Tina asked casually.

"My friend?" I echoed stupidly. Oh. Mick. "Hopefully not. He's got other things to do than witness my gracelessness."

"Shame. The alpha is fun to look at." Tina smiled as she ate her sandwich.

That he was, I couldn't argue that. I *wouldn't* argue that. Nor could I stop my mind from wandering to the condom sitting in my desk drawer. What was it about that damn wolf that got under my skin the way he did? I shoved more of my sandwich in my mouth to keep from talking.

"They are talking about the boss," Crowley said suddenly. "No names yet, but the chatter is floating that the boss won't be happy. They've made some vague references to two other people, but still no names or what roles they are playing."

I chewed quickly and took a swig of my soda to wash it down. "Are you telling me someone indeed hired the ghosts?"

Crowley nodded and swallowed the bite he had taken. "Sure sounds that way."

"Then it has to be those real estate punks," Tina snarled. "Did they think we would scare that easily?"

"There are two females and a male they are speaking about in reference to the job," Crowley continued, ignoring Tina. "One of those has to be the boss. I'm not sure whether it's one of the females or the male, though. Man, these ghosts are rude." Crowley didn't elaborate on that last part.

"Tell that fat fucker I'm on to him," I growled quietly to Crowley.

Deloris snickered. "That ass is a coward. Should have seen how fast he disappeared when I shifted."

"To be fair, you scared the hell out of me too, and I don't scare easily." I wasn't taking the ghost's side; Deloris was just that scary.

"You didn't run," Tina pointed out kindly.

Deloris cackled. "She flew!"

Even Crowley tried to hide his smile at that one. Whatever. Deloris scared whatever was in that damn chair more than she had me. I had enough pride left in me to

89

acknowledge that, even if it was silently.

I finished eating my sandwich and crunched noisily on the chips, darting my eyes around the yard. I was in my no fucks given zone. Dusk was descending upon us, and who knew how long these jerks would wait before materializing or start speaking about something that would clue me in on who was behind this.

Chapter Ten

Tina was corralling the horse she called Z into the barn for the night while Crowley and I walked around in the fading light. There wasn't a purpose to us doing this; we were more making ourselves seen than anything.

"There's something else here," Crowley told me after a few minutes. "I can sense it. Despair."

"Human or spectral?" I wondered out loud.

"Humanoid, and coming from that direction." Crowley waved his hand towards the barn. "There's something I'm missing. It feels like a cactus poking at my brain."

I didn't ask how he knew what that would feel like; some things were better left unsaid. Tina mentioned that Zahbaar was sensitive; maybe Crowley was picking up on something the horse felt. I wasn't going to discount anything.

We had circled the house and were waltzing past the garden when Tina surfaced from the barn but didn't pull the door closed. We slowly meandered in her direction, acting like we were here for some downtime and out for a nightly stroll.

"It's warm tonight," Tina explained, seeing me glance at the open door. "Leaving it open will allow some airflow through there. The horses are enclosed in their stalls; they won't get out."

"How have they been acting since all this started?" Crowley paused his walking until Tina was beside him.

"They sense things. Z has been acting a little odd in the barn, but I haven't seen any ghosts go in there." Tina shrugged. "Last night had them agitated with all the noise."

"Sorry," I mumbled to her.

"No need to apologize. You didn't cause it." Tina latched the gate behind us.

"I did. That wouldn't have happened if I hadn't been here unannounced." I fully owned my part in the fiasco.

Crowley rolled his eyes heavily and shook his head. "The one you called a fat fucker just came up to me and said boogedy-boo in my ear. Where did someone dig these ghosts up? That was about the most pathetic attempt I have seen in all my years."

I snorted. "Truly sad. Though, I can't say it surprises me. Can you see the imbecile? He looks like a joke." I was provoking again.

"The one in a wife-beater?" Tina joined in. "Worst ghost ever."

A wicked gleam popped into Crowley's eyes that told me it was working. "Hah! Risa isn't fat; she's curvy and voluptuous. Nice try, though."

Anger nicked at my nerves, and I frowned. Yeah, my ass was round, and I had boobs. Still, that was a cheap shot, picking on a woman's weight; idiot. Magic prickled my fingertips with a feeling I hadn't felt before. Maybe my internal talk had done some good after all.

Honestly, I wasn't sure what would happen if I released it, and I was debating the wisdom in doing so when a rock came flying at my face. "Sticks and stone," I chirped and aimed my fingers in the direction the rock had appeared. An unholy goose shriek filled the air, causing the

92

horses to react and draw Tina's attention.

"Cheese and rice!" Crowley shouted in surprise. "It was like that scene in the ghost movie where the marshmallow thing exploded! Where they hay-ell have you been hiding that power?" Crowley slapped his hands over his ears and looked distressed for a moment, his eyes bugging out.

"What's wrong?" I worriedly looked him over.

"Holy frog damnation!" Crowley shook his head. "You obliterated that assclown, and now they are all talking up a storm, freely offering all sorts of information. Shut it!" Crowley yelled out to the seemingly empty yard. "If you can't take turns talking, I'm gonna set her loose on all of ya!"

Tina gave me an appreciative smile. "Now that's girl power. I wonder if we could make a bullet out of that?"

Chapter Eleven

One by one, Crowley started conversing with the suddenly talkative ghosts. The magic hadn't left my fingers, whatever it was, and when he gestured to me by waving his fingers, I let it loose where he pointed. I guess those ghosts were giving him attitude.

"Watch out!" Crowley's sudden shout was about two seconds too late.

Something slammed into me, knocking me flat on my back. The rifle Tina had been leaning on with the barrel pointed to the ground went flying, toppling Tina over in the process. Both of us sat there stunned for a moment before leaping to our feet and taking up defensive postures.

"What the hell was that, Crowley?" I called out, watching around me for signs of movement.

"A spelled shifter!" came his swift reply.

"Spelled with what?" Tina paused and picked up the rifle.

"Invisibility," I guessed. I watched the grass we were standing on for blades to bend and pointed them out. Tina raised the rifle and fired off a shot, making Crowley dive for the ground. "I thought there were only ghosts here."

I saw a splatter of blood, heard a grunt, and figured Tina had grazed whoever was attacking us. Then the grass leading toward the barn started to bend, and we heard thudding footsteps. Automatically, I followed them, Tina, right behind me with her rifle at the ready.

Crowley scurried after us. "A gorgon is the boss. She promised resurrection to the ghosts through a necromancer, also a female. But they started talking about a male that was doing something on the property that was bad over here near the barn. I'm going to go out on a limb and say that was the shifter that slammed into you."

"What kind of shifter?" I demanded, my anger building fast. I was going to have it out with Mick if a wolf just attacked me.

Tina's rifle got flung from her hand again, and her surprised shout stopped me. I tuned my senses into everything around me and reached for my magic. The feeling that burned against my fingers wasn't the same energy that had exploded the ghosts.

"Go protect the house, or I'll have her exterminate you!" Crowley yelled at the ghosts. "They said it is a rat."

Tina gaped at Crowley. "A rat?" she repeated. "A rat shifter is doing something on my property near the barn? Is it related to the gorgon trying to run me out of here? Because for damn sure I am going to shoot and kill every single rat I see."

"Um, you already got his friend. I don't believe the two are related. I think these are two separate issues. The gorgon is a real estate agent, but one of the ghosts thinks she is working for someone else. The isolated property with beach access is what they were after to run whatever operation they have going. The rat is something else."

I knew it. Wiley had to be behind the gorgon. "Get the gorgon's name and the necromancer's name. The necromancer has to be registered with the council." I snapped the instructions out to Crowley, and he didn't argue once with my aggressive tone, bless the man.

Suddenly, Tina shifted into one of those pookas that

became utterly terrifying, and her eyes glowed red. I was going to have nightmares about this. Her mane looked like it was made of flames, and her tail became a burning whip that sliced through the air. I grew a healthy respect for pookas in that instant.

Hooves thudded into the ground with a force unexpected for Tina's standard slight frame. "Die, you rat scum!" A voice boomed from the horse's mouth, its nostrils flaring wildly. I might have peed a little when she reared back and slammed her hooves down on the grass again, leaving gigantic indentations.

The second time she did that, I heard the sound of wood splintering, and despite the growing trepidation the beast brought out in me, I moved forward to see what caused that noise. But, to my embarrassment, I was standing on the fractured wood, and under the pressure of my weight, it caved, dropping me into a dark hole.

Chapter Twelve

The jarring impact of my body on hard compacted earth didn't feel so great. I couldn't see anything, but wherever I was, it smelled awful. The sound of scurrying and movement penetrated the painful buzz in my ears. Tina needed to come down here with her rifle if the sound was any indication of the number of rats in this space. Probably relatives of the shifter.

I slowly stood and checked to see if anything broke in this newest tumble into trouble. Quite a few creaks issued from my protesting bones, and two steps into the darkness brought me back down to my knees as I tripped over something: correction, someone.

I flung my arms out in front of me to break my fall and encountered flesh on my right and earth on my left. I grunted in pain and tried to roll to keep from crushing whatever unfortunate soul was down here with me.

"Sorry," I called out and received no response. "Come on, magic; I need a light source." My crazy muttering felt like the darkness swallowed it. My magic finally sparked to life, and a light orb blossomed. My heart stopped as I took in the scene.

"Crowley? Can you hear me?" I shouted frantically.

"Yeah! Are you okay?" Crowley's distant voice answered me.

"Get Mick here now!" I practically screamed. "I found Maggie!"

I bent forward and checked for a pulse, finding a weak and thready one; I breathed a sigh of momentary relief. Then a man appeared as the invisibility spell wore off. This time my defenses reacted instantly and froze him before he could tackle me again. I wasn't sure how long the magic would hold him, but if I knew Mick, he'd be here quickly.

I scanned the unconscious Maggie as best as possible to see if there was anything I could do immediately to help her and found nothing. I stroked her arm and cooed nonsensical words at her until I heard sirens and Mick dropping down the hole.

I thought he would go to Maggie the moment he spotted her, and instead, he squatted in front of me and ran those animalistic eyes over me. His finger caressed the side of my face and came away with blood, and his eyes flashed yellow.

"You're hurt," Mick growled. "Where?"

My body vibrated with a desire to answer the possessiveness in his voice. I honestly had no idea where I was hurt. "Don't worry about me. Get Maggie out of here. The frozen dick over there is a rat shifter that tackled Tina and me. He might be who is behind this."

With more gentleness than I could have imagined, Mick leaned forward to kiss my forehead sweetly. Then, he moved swiftly and picked Maggie up, cradled her, and yanked on the rope I hadn't seen drop, and got pulled up. A few moments later, he dropped back down with a cop.

He picked me up, startling me, and got us pulled out of the hole. "The gorgon and necromancer are being arrested as we speak. Crowley gave me the names. Two cases in one shot; nice job, Risa. I'll be in touch once we figure out more about what happened with Maggie. You deserve to know." Mick turned and left with the pack healer and Maggie.

I tore my eyes away from him, confused about the feelings washing through me, and saw Tina smirking. I shook my head and fought the smile trying to surface.

"Well, you did the job!" Tina crowed happily.

"Kind of accidentally. Are you okay? You weren't hurt, were you?" I glanced her over quickly.

"Right as rain. Thank you for everything. Rest assured, I am going to be hunting rats more vehemently now. What an asshole, hiding that poor girl on my property," Tina clucked her tongue in anger, then broke out in laughter. "I won't ever forget boogedy-boo either."

I chuckled. "Me neither. By the way, you are scarier than your grandma. Pretty sure you made me pee—I'm gonna call you pooka-boo."

Book 8
Knock Me Up

Chapter One

Once again, I, Risa Sanders, find myself getting spoken about publicly, not that I wasn't before. I owned my own supernatural, paranormal investigative agency. That alone gets me talked about often. Only, this time, the things said were all excellent. It was eerie, and it should have made me happy, but instead, I felt annoyed.

Not too long ago, during a case where I investigated a haunted house, I inadvertently solved a missing person case I had taken on for the local wolf pack. In doing so, tongues were waggling about how smart and dedicated I was.

The part that annoyed me was that I am the same person I was before that case landed on my desk. It took finding a missing person for people to realize I'm not some dumb blonde floozy acting like I had skills?

I huffed out a sigh and tried to refocus my thoughts on the ridiculous person in front of me, asking if I could find their lost knickknack from seventy years ago. I was standing in the middle of a grocery store aisle wanting the bar of chocolate the inconsiderate person was blocking from my reach.

I knew it would be rude to shove them out of the way, but I can honestly say I've given the idea some reasonable consideration. I was pretty confident that my hair was changing color with my growing irritation because the man kept flicking his eyeballs to my lustrous locks with fascination alight in his beady rat eyes.

Obviously, my girl's weekend didn't do the trick of taking the cynicism out of my life. I didn't have the power of psychometry, and all I wanted was that damn chocolate bar that was so close but blocked by crazy.

I sighed. I knew I was mentally too hard on the guy. I was tired, ready for a break from the madness my life had turned into, and I needed to get laid something fierce. However, I wasn't prepared for taking the step to make that happen because I knew it would open Pandora's Box on my unlucky ass.

"Anyway, thanks for listening," the old guy patted my arm and blessedly moved away from the chocolate.

Guilt twinged in my belly since I hadn't listened to anything the man said. I only disappeared inside my train wreck of a brain. I was *that* asshole today. I did my best to shrug it off, snatched up the chocolate bar, and grabbed an extra, just in case one wasn't enough.

I only gave a brief glance at the booze the next aisle over. I'd drank enough over the weekend to last me a lifetime. Okay, not really, but it had sure felt like it. I wasn't young anymore. That ship sailed a couple of hundred years ago.

I paid for my chocolate and rushed to my waiting Jeep. I made eye contact with precisely zero people, kept my head down, and didn't look up until I was locked inside my faithful companion with her engine purring.

I pulled out of the parking lot and headed to my office. Before I had left for my girl's weekend, I was supposed to have met a new client or a potential client, but she had never shown up. Well, to be fair, she had, only it was after I had left. It was possible I might have been a touch impatient that day.

Thankfully, the woman was kind and held no grudge for my blunders, and she was coming to meet with me to discuss her issue. Plus, bonus, she had a British accent, and I liked listening to her. The episode with the chocolate blocker put me close to being late for my appointment with her—which was nothing more than a justification for my speeding through town like a starving banshee chasing its next meal.

I arrived at my office with five minutes to spare and ran into the building to get my door unlocked and to try and look somewhat professional. Lately, that was getting more difficult to accomplish, and I could only partially blame my magical puberty.

I tore open the chocolate bar and stuffed a large chunk of it into my mouth while I stashed the other in the drawer with the condom Mick had delivered. I swear I flushed hot enough to make that chocolate a fondu at the images that flooded my mind. I might have even drooled some of that gooey chocolate down my chin. Oh yeah, I'm professional, all right.

About the time the chocolate endorphins kicked in, there was a light knock at my office door, and a petite little woman walked in. She looked right at me and stifled a tiny laugh, then pointed to her face in the universal sign of 'hey stupid, you are wearing your food on your face.'

I wasn't even sure at this point that I could appear more disorganized or unworthy of her business. Calling myself a hot mess would be an understatement. In a move that could only make matters worse, I reached my arm across and wiped my face with my sleeve.

With a defeated sigh, I dropped to my devil chair without a care in the world. An unholy sound rang through my office like it was on a loudspeaker. The only way I could think to describe it would be a whoopie cushion on meth after eating a week's worth of bean meals, with some

107

broccoli, cabbage, and Brussel sprouts thrown in for good measure.

To add insult to injury for my battered pride, the casters on the chair all broke off, like a hippo had stepped on a popsicle stick house held together with a strand of hair.

Spewing curses like an out-of-control firehouse, I leaped up. I kicked the offending chair across the office, momentarily forgetting that I had a proper and dainty audience that probably wasn't used to this type of behavior.

"We all have those kinds of days, love," the little woman told me. "Though that mix of pink and orange hair is quite unique and not the same color it was when I walked in."

I snorted. "I wish I could say it was just one of those days. Instead, it's one of those lives," I corrected the woman. "Come on in; I'm the only one in peril here."

The itty-bitty woman walked in and sat in one of the old plastic chairs. She was so small her feet didn't touch the ground. She had beautiful green eyes and short spiky light brown hair and wore jeans and a sweater, which looked like kid's clothes.

"Thank you. I'm Rhiannon. I called about a problem I'm having with being stalked," Rhiannon began. "How much do you know about Wales?"

"Well, they are the biggest marine mammals," I stated, feeling somewhat stupid I didn't know more.

A tinkling laugh erupted from Rhiannon that sounded musical and enthralled me. "My apologies, I should have clarified, Wales, the country."

I'm pretty sure my hair colored me stupid; my flushed cheeks only enforced it. "Oh, you're Welsh? I automatically assumed British."

"You aren't wrong. Wales is a part of Britain. To

answer your question, though, yes, I am Welsh. I moved here forty years ago because of this creature. To be more accurate, my father moved me here. My sister still resides in Wales, though both of my parents have passed on," Rhiannon informed me.

"I'm sorry to hear that," I answered automatically, sounding trite.

"Thank you," Rhiannon dipped her head in acknowledgment. "There was an entire colony of us pixies that lived in the city of Varteg. It's a small town near Pontypool. I'm aware that you probably have no idea where that is; however, I like to give the complete story. My father was a coal miner and saved enough money to send one of his children here to escape the clutches of a Coblynau. He sent my sister to live with one of his siblings."

I wasn't following the story entirely. I became purely lost in the accent. "What now?"

"Coblynau," Rhiannon repeated. "I'll get to that. Gethin and I came here to try and put us out of reach. It didn't work. A Coblynau followed me."

"Gethin?" I could pronounce that one and wrote it down. "Who is the other one?"

"Coblynau," Rhiannon said slowly, pronouncing it slowly, so it sounded like cob-la-nigh. "Not a who, a what."

"Forgive my ignorance. I haven't heard of Coblynau before," I apologized, doing my best not to butcher the word.

"They knock," Rhiannon replied with an exasperated tone. "Relentless knocking. It's enough to drive me bloody mad!"

I rapped my knuckles on my desk in an automatic reaction and felt instantly awful when Rhiannon flinched and gave me a crazy look. "Sorry," I muttered, silently cursing myself.

Rhiannon closed her eyes a moment, then went on.

109

"My dad was a coal miner. One night, a Coblynau began to knock on the ore. It startled my dad, and he followed the sound and saw the blasted creature. Only about a foot and a half tall, they look like what Americans would call goblins. Ugly, they are. There have been legends over the centuries that Coblynau sometimes helps miners find good veins, and when my dad spotted him, he pointed out an unnoticed vein."

Okay, I was following now. "This creature helped your father discover more of what he was mining."

Rhiannon nodded her head. "He did. It worked out very well for my father, and he got a promotion because of it. The Coblynau figured my father was going to reward him for the help, and when he didn't, the Coblynau became vindictive."

"How so?" I asked, propping my head on my hand as if that would help me understand.

"He'd follow my dad home, knock on the walls of the house at all hours of the night. We all grew sleep-deprived, irritable, and it affected our school work. My sister would misbehave in class. I would fall asleep at my desk," Rhiannon explained. "We even moved."

"Wow, that's extreme." I'd have squashed the beast like a bug.

"We got ostracized by the pixie community," Rhiannon hung her head in shame. "No one would associate with us in fear that the Coblynau would terrorize them as well. Spiteful creature. He believed my dad owed him, and only on the promise of a piece of land, did the Coblynau relent from the knocking on the house walls."

"Your father had to give up land?" I asked incredulously.

Rhiannon shrugged. "Once the knocking stopped, my father sent my sister off to a relative, and he saved all his money to send me here to safety. What we never knew was that the Coblynau had threatened to take us and sell us to workhouses. I don't know if he ever got land from my father or not. My suspicion is he didn't, which is why he 's here now and knocking on the walls of my home."

"Are these Coblynau violent? Are you in danger?" I wondered immediately.

"I want to say no, but the truth is I don't know. I am not unprotected. I have Gethin," Rhiannon answered bluntly.

"Is that your husband?" I asked.

"No. Gethin is my dragon," Rhiannon smiled innocently.

Chapter Two

To continue my unprofessional streak, I sat in my office in stunned silence and stared at my new prospective client as if she were crazy. "Did you just say your dragon?" I finally managed to say.

Rhiannon grinned. "I sure did. Gethin has been my companion since he was a dwt thing." She held her hands up about eight inches apart.

I was beginning to think that Rhiannon needed to get sent out for a drug test. I've met a couple of dragon shifters, and they were nowhere near eight inches big, even as small children or babies. I'd even seen a full-blooded dragon after birth, and it was near horse-sized.

Rhiannon, seeing my disbelief, grinned even wider. "You've seen the Welsh flag, correct?"

I blinked a few times slowly, trying to follow her train of thought. "The white and green flag with a red dragon?"

"That's the one. Gethin is one of the last surviving Welsh red dragons. He was the runt of the litter, but you'd never know that seeing him now," Rhiannon told me proudly. "Gethin talks to me telepathically, and he's eager to roast the Coblynau. Only, we can't find him."

I was back to the slow blinking of my eyes. "You want me to find this creature so your dragon can roast him for dinner?"

"Not quite, though Gethin would probably answer that in the affirmative," Rhiannon laughed. "I want him to leave me alone and let go of this vendetta. If that doesn't work, then sure, I'd be willing to let Gethin have a go at him. The Coblynau isn't big enough to be considered dinner; it would be more akin to a pre-appetizer."

An unladylike snort burst out of me. "Well, that was honest."

"It was," Rhiannon sighed. "I'm at the end of my rope here. I'm not normally murderous."

I get annoyed by the sound of my ice cube maker dropping ice cubes in my freezer. I couldn't imagine listening to knocking all day and night. I'd be homicidal too. However, my mind was still stuck on having a pet dragon.

"Where's Gethin now?" I boldly asked, wanting to see him.

"Do you believe it's possible to help me?" Rhiannon countered.

"I'll do my best," I promised.

"Gethin is hiding outside. He flew me here," Rhiannon announced. "We live upon the top of the mountain for privacy."

I pulled a contract out of my drawer and slid it across the desk. "Here is my contract. The fees listed here," I tapped the paper with my pen. "If you'd like to hire me, fill in your address, and sign here." I pointed to the bottom of the paper and laid the pen down on top.

Rhiannon read over the contract carefully, asking questions about vague wording, made a few notations that I agreed to, then signed. "Knock me up around nine tomorrow morning," she stated.

I blankly stared at her a moment. "I'm positive that you don't mean what I think that means because I don't have the equipment necessary to do what I think that means."

A magical tinkling laugh filled my office. "I sometimes forget that phrases are different here. Come by around nine," Rhiannon rephrased her statement. "You know, in hotels, how you ask to get woken up at a certain time? That's what that means."

"I learned new things today. Grateful for the explanation, yet I still found it funny. Thank you for that opportunity. The knocking up will commence at nine."

I walked Rhiannon outside, not because I wanted to see Gethin; uh, that was a lie. That was precisely why walked her outside. Unfortunately, all I saw was the same old, dilapidated parking lot I always saw. Feeling let down, forced a smile on my face.

"Safe travels home," I told Rhiannon with a note of cheer I didn't feel.

Pixies were notoriously mischievous creatures. I had no reason to believe that Rhiannon wasn't the same way, given the smile on her face, despite her outwardly sweet, dainty, and innocent appearance. The fact that she wanted to let Gethin roast this Coblynau was a dead giveaway on that, not that I blamed her.

"Is this your Jeep?" Rhiannon pointed to my vehicular baby.

"Yeah. This old gal has gotten me through a lot of things," I smiled fondly at the red vehicle that I had formed an odd attachment to over the years.

Imagine my surprise when said Jeep rose about five feet off the ground and dangled like it was a child's toy. It shouldn't have surprised me, given the cases, creatures, and things I've dealt with; however, the moment made me realize that I should start doing Kegel exercises again lest any leaks sprang.

I took three steps forward and slammed into an invisible moving wall. It was only by sheer luck that my boobs hit first instead of my face. I flung my hands out in front of me, and to my utter shock and delight, I encountered hard scales as one would find on a dragon.

No lie, I squealed like a child going down a slide for the first time into a fluffy pile of cotton candy. "Why can't I see him?" I squeaked out in a very un-Risa-like voice.

Rhiannon giggled and covered her mouth. "Gethin said he appreciates getting felt up. He has invisibility magic. He doesn't want to scare people. He also doesn't want to be hunted either because of his rarity."

An unwelcome thought of the town's newest resident, and a shady one at that, popped into my head. "Good call. There's a person here who would steal him and sell him," I admitted.

A huff and two smoky steam clouds alerted me to the dragon's unhappiness at hearing that. I turned around to look at Rhiannon, but she, too, had disappeared. Gethin's scales were still under my hands, and I was still stroking the dragon.

"Uh, Rhiannon?" I asked quietly.

"I'm on Gethin," Rhiannon's soft answer floated down to me. "We'll see you in the morning."

The downdraft from the wings was enough to make me feel like gravity had increased and was trying to push me into the ground. Just as suddenly, it was gone, and I stood alone in the parking lot of a bad part of town grinning like a damn idiot because I touched a dragon.

Chapter Three

O kay, Mom, why am I going with you up the side of a mountain?" Jameson, my youngest son, asked me.

"Because you love your aging mother, and if I get roasted like a pig on a spit, you might need to heal me," I truthfully told my son.

"I'm gonna need more than that, Mom," Jameson replied testily.

"I felt up a dragon?" I offered, knowing it would only frustrate him more and add more questions to the growing list I was sure was in his head.

"You are insufferable," Jameson finally growled with an eye roll so intense I felt it.

"You are my backup on this case. I'm looking for a Coblynau, and I am not sure that I will find him on my own. Your particular DNA might come in handy," I relented and told Jameson. He was half-angel, half-demon, and could spot creatures of light or dark fairly easily.

"You are looking for a what? And what did you mean you felt up a dragon?" Jameson asked, crossing his arms.

It didn't pass my notice that my son's arms had grown thicker with muscle. Jameson was a handsome man, and I was immensely proud of him. Yet, I still wondered who it was that had made him decide to work out and beef up. I knew better than to ask.

"Coblynau," I answered, pronouncing it slowly. "A creature from Wales that knocks all the time. Supposed to be about a foot and a half tall, and I was told they resemble what Americans think a goblin looks like."

I almost laughed at the expression on my son's face. It was a single blink at first, then a series of rapid blinks as his face settled into a mask of intrigue and shock. Poor Jameson couldn't tell which emotion to land on after that.

"And the client has a Welsh red dragon as security and a pet, and even cooler, the dragon, Gethin is his name, has invisibility magic. I walked right into him yesterday and then proceeded to feel him up. Probably not the best move on my part, but Rhiannon said he enjoyed it," I added helpfully.

This time, when Jameson blinked, his eyes stayed closed. "I don't know why I ask."

I bit back a laugh and continued driving my trusty Jeep up the narrow, winding, dirt road that hopefully was the right path to where Rhiannon lived with Gethin. My excitement of seeing a rare red Welsh dragon made me speed.

"Mom! Get your head out of the clouds! Or out of your ass, wherever it is," Jameson shouted as the Jeep skidded sideways on a switchback. "Mick or Danny should be with you," my son muttered.

"Danny cheated on me," I snapped out. "Mick," I started, then stopped. Jameson didn't need to know my frustrations with the alpha wolf. "Mick has better things to do than babysit me."

Jameson snorted. "Yet he always seems to be near when disaster strikes."

Okay, my son had a point. Mick might tend to be possessive or controlling when it's something he wants or feels is his. We had a few discussions recently about the stalker-ish behavior, and in my opinion, nothing got resolved. Whatever.

I was going to get to meet a dragon who could go invisible. Maybe Gethin was single. I could have him singe the hair right off the bossy wolf. I bet he wouldn't be so intimidating as an oversized hairless mutt.

Jameson fell silent for the rest of the drive, and when we came to a dead-end, he was reluctant to get out of the Jeep. When he finally closed the door, he looked over the hood at me. "Is there seriously a dragon?"

I couldn't help it. I belted out a hearty laugh. "There is; I wasn't lying. Are you telling me you are scared?" I was a horrible mother because I found that funny and was going to exploit it. Especially after his experimental potion, he'd had me drink to help try and tame my burgeoning magical powers.

"Those words never left my lips," Jameson protested a bit too much.

I toned down my snickering and began to follow the stone steps that led up through a thickly wooded area. almost missed the doorbell camera mounted on one of the branches. I wondered how Rhiannon got a signal to run it and then remembered we lived in a magical town.

Thankfully, the path wasn't too long, and when a beautiful stone-carved house built into the mountain came into view, I paused, and my breath caught. I'd never seen something like that in person before, and it was stunning. I expected a cottage.

"Holy shit!" Jameson exclaimed, stopping next to me. "Is your client royalty?"

"She's a pixie whose father was a coal miner," I said on an exhale. "I wonder who built this."

"I'm willing to bet that it's been here longer than we have," Jameson replied in wonder. His fear was momentarily forgotten.

That is until a deafening roar rumbled the ground under our soles and shoved us back a few feet. My son visibly trembled and became a few shades paler as he stepped behind me. I wasn't as quick to laugh this time since Gethin had about made me piss myself. *Kegels, start them now*, I reminded myself.

"Uh, Gethin?" my voice shook more than I wanted. "Remember me? Risa? Rhiannon hired me to help with the Coblynau. She's expecting me."

Another roar tore through the air with enough force to turn my bowels to a dangerous liquid state. Jameson yelped behind me.

"Mom! Did you fart?" he had the audacity to ask me.

"Rude. No. I did not." At least I didn't think I had.

"Gethin, let them through," Rhiannon's voice carried from the massive stone porch. "Sorry, Risa. He wasn't expecting you to have someone with you. The Coblynau has Gethin all out of sorts."

"Would it help if I offered to stroke him again?" I offered weakly, but hopefully. "This is my son, Jameson. He's helpful in finding and identifying magical beings."

Amused sounding huffs and puffs of smoke materialized about halfway between Jameson and me and the porch where Rhiannon waited for us. We'd have to walk right by an invisible dragon that could incinerate us to dust and had a powerful enough roar to shake a mountain. Jameson might not move from where he stood.

I hoped that it passed Rhiannon's notice that Jameson hadn't figured out a gigantic invisible dragon had stood in front of us the entire time we gawked at her home like starstruck tourists viewing the queen in a state of undress.

"We're here to knock you up!" I tried again to ease Gethin's mind.

"What the actual fuck, Mom?" Jameson hissed

behind me; his voice was aghast.

I'd lost my mind. It was utterly apparent that I was not the only one who hadn't heard that Welsh turn of phrase before. "Chill, child of mine. I'm not offering you up to impregnate my client."

Oh man, I was going to lose it. Hysterical laughter began to bubble up inside, and I was grateful that before it was released, the air in front of me shimmered. A magnificent, iridescent red-scaled, massive dragon materialized.

"Hot damn, I'm in love," I blurted out with no shame.

Chapter Four

Gethin liked me. I could just feel it deep in my bones. Or it could be that it was relief that I still had bones and wasn't a pile of charred flesh in front of a meticulous and pristine stone house carved into a mountain.

I boldly took a few steps forward, and when I wasn't stopped, I kept going. I could sense Jameson directly behind me, not willing to be left alone with the gorgeous creature. As I neared where Gethin held his position, I reached out to brush my fingers over his scales again. He didn't stop me, which told me I was right; he loved me too.

Rhiannon began to laugh that wonderful laugh of hers, and I wondered if she'd adopt me and let me live here and swoon over her dragon. Better not ask. She didn't need to know how pathetic I was.

"Mom," Jameson's whispered and urgent warning was less than half a second too late.

I heard the knocking sound, and Gethin reacted instantly. Rhiannon's shout got lost in the sound of the grumble that came from the dragon. Like the sound of a thousand dump trucks unloading monolithic stones at the same time.

A stream of the hottest fire I had ever been near shot past me, singeing the hair on my arms and turning a giant redwood tree to nothing more than smoldering cinders in the blink of an eye. A second later, a thick red spiked tail came swinging toward me.

Jameson jumped, and I was not quick enough or probably nimble enough to pull that move off, which meant that I got a solar plexus full of dragon tail in full combat swing that pinned me to a pine tree that bowed under the pressure.

A disturbed laugh filled the air, eerie enough to make those burned hairs on my arm stand straight up and then more knocking.

"Okay," I grunted with my remaining oxygen. Gethin's tail moved only a fraction of an inch, but it was enough to get some air into my bruised lungs. "I agree with you. Roast the assclown and pick your teeth with his bones."

Jameson and Rhiannon rushed over to me as Gethin let out an amused snort and released me from his hold. I crumpled to the ground in a heap of uncoordinated limbs and waited patiently for Jameson to skirt around the dragon to get to me.

"Are you alright?" Rhiannon asked me as she shot a glare at Gethin.

"Once my son gets over his fear and heals me, I'll be fine," I promised with a glare similar to Rhiannon's aimed at Jameson.

Rhiannon scurried over Gethin's tale and perched beside me. "Go find that Coblynau," she snapped at Gethin. "Give the boy some space to help his mother."

I swear, I could hear Jameson's butt cheeks slam together when the dragon moved. Jameson pointed to a spot between two trees. "He's there."

Another molten hot stream of fire shot through the air with precision I didn't know was possible. Jameson squeaked, Rhiannon shook her head in aggravation, and I sighed happily.

124

"Oh, Gethin, you stole my heart," I swooned.

"Your hair is a rainbow," Jameson told me with an eye roll.

He knelt, placed his hands on my arm, and fixed whatever had gotten damaged. Except for the burned patches of hair on my arm, those remained as a reminder that loving a dragon had consequences when knocking happened. Everyone knew that, right?

Rhiannon helped me up and then led us into the stone palace. "When Gethin and I arrived here in town, he headed here immediately after spotting the peak. We happened upon this place, and after some careful searching, we found it vacant and moved in. I probably should have checked to see if anyone owns the place or has rights to it, but there were so many cobwebs, Gethin told me to not worry about it."

Jameson gulped. "He talks?"

"Of course. Gethin is quite intelligent," Rhiannon smiled kindly at Jameson. "I'm Rhiannon." She held out her small dainty hand.

Jameson's hand swallowed hers. "Jameson. I'm Risa's youngest son. It's a pleasure to meet you, Rhiannon. Your home is amazing."

At least I raised a polite child even if he was afraid of dragons.

"I can't claim credit for this place," Rhiannon reminded him. "I'm merely a squatter here."

"You made it a home," Jameson argued. "Yes, the stonework is stunning, but I am speaking to the cozy feel of the place once you are inside."

What a charmer; I rolled my eyes. Cutting their conversation short, I broke in. "That was quite the introduction to the Coblynau."

"When we returned home yesterday from our visit, the creature was insufferable. I'm afraid that is why Gethin

125

is so on edge today. We've not had a moment's rest from the antics," Rhiannon told us.

"Is it invisible too?" I wondered.

"No. Coblynau are masters at hiding from sight," Rhiannon informed us with a tired voice. "Gethin would burn the entire forest to the ground trying to find him if I would allow it. Some of those trees out there are several hundred years old and are homes to souls. I can't have them burn."

"That would be a shame," Jameson agreed, with a nervous glance behind him. He cleared his throat. "Uh, where does Gethin go? It doesn't seem like he would fit in here."

"Oh, no. Not in these front rooms," Rhiannon shook her head. "The back of the place is where he stays. There is a hidden cave that allows him access, and the rooms are cavernous."

"May I ask a stupid question?" Jameson paused to wait for Rhiannon's acceptance. "This Coblynau, is that its name?"

"No." Rhiannon got one of those distant stares that saw nothing. "My father never told us Coblynau's name, as names hold power. We only ever called him Coblynau. It always seemed disrespectful to me, demeaning in a way. Though, now, I don't care quite as much since he is hell-bent on driving me mad."

Jameson looked thoughtful for a split second until the floor shook, and that terrified expression settled back on his face. With another vibration through the floor, Rhiannon smiled and refocused her gaze on us.

"Gethin is inside now," she stated.

Chapter Five

After a tour through the stone palace, and yes, I couldn't stop calling it that because of the sheer size of the place. I also wasn't sure how a creature like the Coblynau could knock on the thick stone walls and have it heard. Yet, he managed it since the incessant knocking followed us.

"So annoying," Jameson grumbled.

"Hence Rhiannon hiring me," I reminded him.

"I can't spot the bastard through these walls." Jameson thumped his hand on the wall, and the only sound was the flesh hitting stone. "A couple of times, I picked up on the residual energy he has left behind, but no real signature. I'm not sure I am going to be a help to you, Mom."

I narrowed my gaze on my son. "Are you saying that out of fear because of Gethin?" I knew firsthand how good Jameson was at picking up on magical beings.

Jameson pursed his lips and looked like he was about to argue, then changed his mind. "Maybe partially. But I'm not lying."

"If I may," Rhiannon's voice was unexpected and startled both of us as we had thought we were alone. "Risa, you have immense power. Gethin says he can taste it. I suggest trying to funnel your power through your son;

it might increase his ability to sense Coblynau."

Jameson raised his eyebrows in surprise at the thought and flicked his eyes over to me. "Do you feel stable enough to try that?"

I pinched the bridge of my nose in frustration at Jameson's use of the word stable. "I'm not unstable," I sighed.

"Of course, you aren't, love," Rhiannon cooed gently at me. "I've heard many wonderful things about you from various people."

"I meant your magic, Mom," Jameson's sigh was equally frustrated.

"I know what you meant." It took all my willpower to keep from snapping. The truth was, I didn't know if my magic was stable enough to try something like what Rhiannon suggested. If it went badly, I could seriously harm my youngest son, and that thought terrified me more than Gethin scared Jameson.

"Gethin could help you," Rhiannon offered kindly. "I can't claim to understand your magic or what you can do, but he seems to think you can handle it."

Jameson's face displayed every ounce of skepticism he felt. "My mom's magic is unpredictable. It could likely bring this mountain down on top of us."

Rhiannon looked over at me with empathy on her face. "Late bloomer? I was too. It was a terrible time for me, though Gethin coached me through the worst of it."

"How?" Jameson cocked his head to the side, willing to listen.

"Dragons are made of magic," Rhiannon explained. "He intuitively knows how to wield it to get the desired outcomes. He understands when it's too powerful and how to dilute the wild spurts that cause disasters. Gethin can deflect attacks with his scales, or he can use them to absorb the energy and redirect it."

"Gethin? Will you marry me?" I shouted out into the hallway.

Rhiannon's delighted laughter filled the air. "He said he prefers bachelorhood and playing the field, though he is flattered."

Jameson smirked at me. "Rejected by a dragon. That's a new one."

Rhiannon shook her head at Jameson. "It's not rejection. Gethin doesn't have a human form, and dragons mate for life. Sex with your mother would likely kill her."

With a pinched look, Jameson replied, "Okay. Enough talk about my mother's sex life. Is there a safe place outdoors where we could work on channeling her magic into mine?"

Wait. Was Jameson considering this? "I don't think so, child of mine. It could kill you. Not to mention I could inadvertently obliterate this house."

Rhiannon put her hand on my arm. "I'm willing to risk losing my home if it gets rid of Coblynau. Besides, I believe in you and think you could pull this off spectacularly."

Jeez, I would have a girl crush and a dragon crush if they talked to me that way. Sighing, I looked over at my youngest son. "I understand what Gethin is telling me, but what if it's too much and destroys the conduit? That would be you," I added in case his love for science and experiments got in the way of rational thinking.

"Mom, you'll be my battery," Jameson argued. "In theory, with a backup supply of power running into mine, I'll be able to extend farther and see better. Wouldn't it be worth that to help Rhiannon and Gethin? I mean, think about it. Do we really want a temperamental, overtired, and jumpy dragon on the loose?"

"Jameson," I started, and he cut me off again.

"This could be what we need to understand how to

129

help control your magic and help you use it better instead of trusting it to kick in when you need it—or blowing something up when you get mad. The potion didn't work as we thought it would, and I've been telling you that you need to work with someone."

"That's Gage," I interrupted the little twerp.

"I happen to agree with him," Jameson silenced me with a look. "It will ensure you get to spend more time with Gethin."

"Gethin said he knows a perfect spot," Rhiannon gently put her hand on my arm. "Though I have to admit, the changing hair color is quite fetching and informative. I'm going to guess that your magic is feeding off your emotions."

My irritation was rapidly growing. "Fine." I looked at Jameson, "If I blow you up, I'm going to feed your remains to Gethin."

My idle threat didn't work. Jameson was too excited about trying something new to remember he was terrified of Gethin. My stomach was in knots over the whole thing, though maybe it would go well, and we'd find Coblynau, make Rhiannon's life easier, and ease Gethin's nerves. The possibility existed that it could go the way of utter disaster too.

Chapter Six

I don't know what made Gethin think this area was safe to try something this risky. Trees surrounded us. Those would all become weapons should something go awry. I felt sick.

"I think Coblynau is close," Jameson whispered in my ear. "I can feel something on the fringes of my reach. There, but not close enough for me to identify. I think this was Gethin's hope. That we draw the bugger out."

I understood the logic, but I still bent at the waist and hurled up all the food I'd eaten since I was five in a fabulous display of confidence in my abilities.

"Oh, dear," Rhiannon said sympathetically. "I'll go fetch you a glass of water." I heard her dainty little feet pattering away.

Jameson cringed and moved away from me. "Nerves?" he asked.

Gethin chose that moment to reveal himself, and what I assumed was a dragon grin. It was both frightening and captivating at the same time. He huffed once and then spat out a fireball that incinerated my smelly deposit of waste to nothing.

Jameson squeaked again and leaped about six feet behind me. "See?" he called out, his voice wavering. "No harm, no foul."

Beyond embarrassed, I gave Gethin a grateful nod, wishing I could communicate with him. He chose that moment to lower his four legs and get close to the ground, and held a wing out to me. I wasn't sure what he wanted me to do, so I moved closer and shook it like I would a hand.

I heard Rhiannon laughing behind me. I turned around, and she handed me a glass of water that I gratefully downed before handing it back.

"Gethin wants you to climb up onto his back. He said this is how you will learn to trust him, that he doesn't wish you harm," Rhiannon relayed to me. "To learn how to use your magic, you need to trust him."

"No way in hell!" Jameson blurted out. "Mom, it would be insane for you to climb on a dragon's back."

"That's how I get places," Rhiannon placed a small hand on Jameson's arm. "If he wanted to hurt Risa, he would have."

That statement didn't inspire the confidence she intended it to, and I bit my tongue so I wouldn't laugh when Jameson's face pinched up with an argument that he forced himself to swallow.

"Mom, do you have paper and a pencil? While you are trying to kill yourself with a dragon, I will jot down a few ideas I have on how to help channel the magic. I don't want to forget, and I figured watching the suicide run might make it all disappear in a puff of dragon fire," Jameson smarted off to me.

"Fresh out, sorry. There might be some back in the Jeep," I took a tentative step toward Gethin, with Rhiannon nodding at me to continue.

"No bother, I have some. I'll get a rubber too," Rhiannon offered after seeing me approach Gethin's wing.

Jameson gaped at Rhiannon, and I almost pitched forward onto Gethin's wing. I was positive that this was another of the sayings that were different between our regions, but witnessing Jameson's expression firsthand was priceless.

"Is the rubber because we knocked you up? At that point, the rubber is pointless." I joked. I immediately began working on Kegels because I felt like holding this type of laughter in would make me pee all over Gethin. I couldn't help it either; I snorted.

Rhiannon narrowed her eyes for a moment, not understanding, then her face lit up with glee. "Oh, my. A rubber is an eraser," she told Jameson. "Not a prophylactic."

Jameson blushed so profoundly red that he almost matched Gethin's scales. If the dragon hadn't raised his wing, I would have slid right off; I laughed so hard. My poor son was far less amused. I'd found his limit: dragons and Welsh phrases.

"I can't heal if you if you fall off a dragon and break your neck!" Jameson shouted at me. "I'd need to call Dad for that."

That was an effective way to shut me up. "Gethin, if a fallen angel named Luca shows up here, fry his ass, then eat it."

Rhiannon snorted, and it made me laugh again. "Gethin said that fallen angels taste better slow-roasted. If they cook too quickly, they taste like brimstone."

I patted Gethin's neck as I straddled my legs over the scales and spiky parts of his neck. My butt slid right between the spikes with no room to spare. With no warning at all, the massive wings flapped, and we rose into the air.

I didn't squeal as Jameson did, but I think I squeaked and hugged the spike in front of me. I glanced down as we rose to see Jameson's face looking apoplectic, his pencil with a rubber hanging uselessly in his hand. So I guess I wouldn't win any mother of the year award.

Gethin chose that moment to do some growl thing that caused vibrations through very sensitive parts of my body that were currently squished up against him. Who needed a man anyway? A ride on a dragon's back was proving to be more effective.

Until a stream of fire shot from Gethin's snout, and he dove into a barrel roll that had me forgetting my second's earlier pleasure. It wasn't an orgasmic scream that punctured the air. It was pure terror. Luckily, the g-force of the motion kept me rooted in place and clinging to a dragon spike for all the good it did me.

"What the hell, dragon?" I shouted fruitlessly. "I thought you wanted me to trust you? Trying to kill me isn't giving me warm fuzzies in the trust department!"

Gethin was a sadist. He flew me through several pee-inducing maneuvers that not even Kegels could help. Hell, not even adult diapers would have helped. The last straw of my sanity snapped when the infuriating dragon dove right into the frigid waters of a mountain lake. He swam through it like a bullet through a watermelon.

The moment we surfaced and rose into the air, my magic reacted, not that it had any effect whatsoever on Gethin; he simply absorbed it. At least he radiated enough heat to dry me, and reluctantly, I had to admit the ice-cold bath washed the evidence away that I'd wet myself. Still, I wasn't happy; however, I did trust him not to let me die.

"Fine, you wicked beast. Put us back down, and we'll do the damned magic funnel thing," I shouted.

Chapter Seven

Y ou smell like urine," was the first thing out of my son's mouth. "Hope you're happy."

I patted his face and said nothing. There wasn't much I could say to that without injuring my pride further after having peed on a dragon. "Let's begin."

Thankfully, Rhiannon said nothing nor gave me a pitying look. I don't know if Gethin told her or not, but I figured she knew. I was thankful she was more polite than my son.

"Gethin said to hold hands. Since you both already have a bond, it shouldn't require more than that," Rhiannon recited, glancing between Gethin and me.

He was probably ratting me out, the beautiful mean beast that he was. I snatched up Jameson's hand and squeezed tightly. His return squeeze comforted me.

"Jameson," Rhiannon looked at him next. "Gethin said to do what you normally do to try and find what you are looking for." Rhiannon turned her eyes to me. "He said for you to picture adding your magic to Jameson's. Visualize his pool of power and just add power to it."

Right. Okay. Pool of power; do *not* remember peeing on Rhiannon's dragon. *Do your Kegels.* I visualized a mud puddle. I'm sure that isn't what Gethin meant, but that is what came to mind. How do I picture adding power to a

135

pool? All I could think of was lightning striking it.

Now, I didn't actually intend for that image to solidify in my mind, yet that is what happened, and Jameson shrieked and yanked his hand from me when my magic zapped him.

"Mom!" Jameson shook his head and flexed his fingers, trying to get movement back into them. "Electrocuting me isn't what she said to do."

Rhiannon's eyes went saucer wide. "Oh, dear. No, love. Try picturing a windmill and a gentle breeze just enough to make the blades turn," Rhiannon suggested, fighting a smile. "He is the windmill, and you are the breeze powering it."

That direction was a little easier to follow, though Jameson was reluctant to hold my hand again. Probably rightly so, too. My magic was bitchy.

"Don't grab my hand until I have the visual in my mind," I directed Jameson. "Do your thing, and I'll do mine. Then we can connect."

Jameson sighed dramatically but didn't argue. I didn't think he wanted to get tasered again. I could feel his magic in the air, the scent of vanilla cupcakes and brimstone. It soothed me, oddly enough. I closed my eyes and slid into a zen-like state.

The picture of the windmill came quickly enough to my mind. It was one of those stone structures, white in color, with four blades that looked like a grid in an X-shape and three windows down the front of it. For not having seen it before, it was a pretty detailed image.

Make the blades move, I told myself. I pictured the wildflowers in the field around it swaying, and when the blades rotated a bit, I reached for Jameson's hand. *Feed the wind to the blades and give Jameson a boost in power.*

I wanted to jump up and down in excitement when my visual windmill blades began to rotate. I was doing it!

136

I cracked open an eye and glanced at Jameson, whose face lit in wonder. "It's working," he whispered. "Great work, Mom. A little more if you can."

Rhiannon was clapping her hands gently, looking like a proud parent of a kid who won the kindergarten spelling bee. If I was honest, I was a tad impressed with myself. I changed my visual to one of a windmill moving along at a nice steady pace, the blades slicing cleanly through the air.

"The mountain," Jameson spoke more loudly this time. "The creature is in the mountain. Forty-five degrees from where I am standing."

Gethin cocked his head to the side and became very still. Rhiannon motioned for us to walk in that direction, and we moved as a unit. Our steps were in total synchronization. Jameson guided us quietly but with an air of confidence.

Everything was smooth until a wolf howl split the air. Closer than I would have liked and altogether too familiar. The image I so carefully held in my mind changed to one of the wind turbines that got used for an alternate energy source, and the blades weren't moving gently; they were spinning like they were caught in a hurricane.

Power surged through my body, directly into Jameson like a live wire. His body bowed, and the trees bent like they were curtseying the queen of the mountain. Gethin's tail swung into my midsection, flinging me directly skyward and up into the air with a crack of my ribs, severing my connection with Jameson.

I get why he did it, but come on, that shit hurt. My fury at Mick kept my mind focused on asking Gethin to char-broil Mick's ass. However, I was still traveling upwards at a rapid pace and had yet to figure out how I would land without shattering all my bones.

Rhiannon to the rescue. Her tiny little pixie body

was flying furiously to catch up to me, and once I was within reach, she yanked on my flailing arm to halt my ascent to the heavens. Pain jolted through my body at the sudden direction change. Rhiannon was much stronger than she appeared.

Math might not be my strong suit, but even I could calculate the odds of Rhiannon's small stature being able to sustain and carry my much larger one, despite her apparent strength. A fact which became evident when we began to fall much quicker than she anticipated, and a look of panic crossed her face.

That was when Gethin crushed my heart. The massive red dragon leaped into the air and caught Rhiannon, batting me out of the way and sending me hurtling toward the earth. Bracing for impact and cursing Gethin, I didn't see the giant wolf until his jaws clamped down on my ankle.

Mick twisted mid-air, so I landed on him rather than the rocky ground that waited for me patiently. I should be grateful to him, but I was angry. Not only that, I didn't have enough oxygen to yell at him because my ribs were jabbing into my lungs. Hello, darkness, you old bastard.

Chapter Eight

An annoying buzz in my ears, followed by a knocking, told me I wasn't dead.

"You might want to leave before she wakes up," I heard Jameson's voice say. "I'm almost finished healing her."

"I found an extra set of clothes in the boot," Rhiannon's voice came next.

What? I didn't have clothes stuffed into a boot. I struggled to get my eyes opened, shoving aside the flash of pain that lit my chest on fire. At least I hoped it was pain, and I wasn't on actual fire.

"Is this revenge for peeing on you?" I croaked out, managing to crack my eyes open a slit.

A wet dog nose shoved into my ear, then I smelled the scent of burning hair and a yelp, followed by a menacing growl. Okay, now I had to get my ass up to see what had happened.

"Easy, Mom," Jameson told me, supporting my back as I sat up.

"Good work, kid. I only feel a little bit of pain now," I grunted and forced my eyes all the way open.

Mick stood about twenty feet away from me, his back haunches smoking and bald, as well as his tail. I broke out into laughter so hard that I saw stars, and I couldn't get oxygen into my freshly healed lungs.

"I'm sorry. Gethin said that you told him to char-broil his ass," Rhiannon informed me with a pink tint to her cheeks. "Those were his words."

"I only thought that," I muttered between hiccups.

Rhiannon shook her head with a smile. "No, they were out loud. He was only trying to help me; he didn't mean to hurt you, so Gethin said he figured he could grant your wish."

I doubled over with laughter again. "Sorry, Mick. You deserve that for distracting me from what I was doing. Thanks for saving me, now go away."

"Told you to leave before she woke up," Jameson replied with a shake of his head.

"Whoa. Jameson. You are glowing." I stared at my son, my laughter gone in an instant.

Rhiannon flitted over and heaved me to my feet. "Come on over here into the trees and change into these clean clothes I got from your boot."

"I don't have clothes in my boot," I pushed Rhiannon away from me slightly. "What's going on?"

"Sorry. The back of your Jeep. Trunk, you call it, I think." Rhiannon held the clothes out to me. "Change, and then we'll figure out what's happening."

I pursed my lips, glanced over to where Mick still stood. He looked funny with a hairless tail. "Don't follow me," I warned.

Glancing down at my clothes, I saw my shirt was blood-soaked and winced. It must have happened when Gethin hit me with his tail. I changed as quickly as I could and walked back to where the other stood.

Rhiannon took my ruined clothes and tossed them away from us, where Gethin cremated them. "Gethin thinks that some of your power remains in Jameson but that it will dissipate over time."

"It doesn't hurt, Mom," Jameson assured me. "I can feel Coblynau now. Hell, I can feel everything. Healing you didn't take any energy at all, either."

Mick growled, low and deep, and took a step closer to me.

"Skedaddle!" I shooed him away.

"His wolf is attached to you," Rhiannon told me with her head tilted to the side. "He's worried you are still in danger."

I sighed and turned. "Mick, go. We'll talk later. I'm working."

"I'll get her home safely, I promise," Jameson added from behind me.

Damn these overbearing, protective males in my life. "I'm capable of taking care of myself!" Sparks flew from my fingertips in a rainbow kaleidoscope of colors. That finally made the wolf move. "Let's finish this."

Jameson once again led the way, altering course along the way as the sought-after creature moved, trying to remain hidden. It was as if there was a spotlight on Coblynau, or a tracking beacon for my son.

Gethin got a little too close to Jameson for his comfort more than a couple of times, and he admonished the dragon in a trembling voice. It was nowhere near the threatening tone I am sure my son intended, and I managed to keep from laughing in his presence at least.

After an hour and thirty-five minutes of zigzagging through the forested mountain, I finally caught a flash of movement and halted my momentum. Jameson silently pointed to a large stone. Before I could move, Rhiannon stopped me with a hand on my arm.

She handed me a long, spindly stick. "Your magic will know what to do with it," she whispered in my ear.

I'm not sure where Gethin and Rhiannon's belief in my magical abilities stemmed from, but it was safe to say that I had my doubts. Without magic, there wasn't a lot I could do with a stick this thin other than use it as a switch and hope it wouldn't break. It wasn't likely the Coblynau would hold still for that.

Regardless, I crept forward using my well-honed skills at remaining silent. Years of practice creeping up to open windows to catch cheating spouses paid off for me in this case.

The stone the Coblynau was hiding behind was about the size of a small car and held several blind spots that I could use to my advantage. Stuffing the stick down the back of my shirt, I dropped to a squat. I crab-walked my way around the side of the stone. I moved in the opposite direction of the minimal noise made by the rest of my party.

It was effortless and the not as clever as he thought Coblynau was peering around that side of the stone, trying to see Rhiannon, Gethin, and Jameson. He should have clued in that one person was missing. Or perhaps he should have paid attention to that sixth sense that told you that you were no longer alone.

I paused to slide the stick out of my shirt, pausing every inch or so to make sure the fabric rustling didn't alert him to my presence. Once it was free, I held it loosely in my hand, staring at it in confusion for a second or thirty.

The ugly little Coblynau grinned evilly and knocked on the rock. The sound grated on my nerves, and I rolled my eyes. *Come on, magic. Do something useful with this twig,* I pleaded internally. Deep down, I didn't want to murder the little punk or let Gethin do it.

To my utter shock, the stick transformed into a rope. A lasso, to be exact. "What the—" my surprised gasp made the Coblynau reel around and stared at me in astonished anger at being caught. Only I didn't know how to use a lasso.

142

The big-nosed, brown-skinned, creepy little man started to scoot backward. "Hey! You little pipsqueak shit, get your ass over here!" I shouted. I raised my arm and flung the rope out in a hopeless gesture. A cowgirl I was not, despite having had a case where I had to round up missing cows.

The loop in the rope fell short, and the Coblynau let out a snicker at my ineptness. Even knowing it was there in front of him, his fright at having Jameson creep up on him from the other side didn't stop the idiot from stepping right into the open loop.

I yanked hard on the lasso and bound the Coblynau's feet in one swift move that impressed me if I did say so myself. And I did; out loud for everyone to hear. I had some dignity to regain after peeing on a dragon while doing Kegels.

I pulled the rope, dragging the Coblynau's obnoxious ass across the ground. "What do you have to say for yourself?"

"This woman owes me land!" the Coblynau shouted, spittle flying from his mouth.

"She owes you nothing," I corrected. Grabbing the little turd by the shirt, I lifted Coblynau right off the ground and dangled him before me. "You had a deal with her father, not her. Death ends all contracts unless you made a deal with the devil. Rhiannon is clearly not the devil."

"The contract was a blood contract. This woman carries her father's blood," the Coblynau struggled to get free, his feet swinging madly, looking to land a kick. Fortunately for me, my arms were longer than his reach, and all he got was air.

"Listen closely, little man," I demanded in a stern tone. "Death ends contracts. Rhiannon owes you nothing," I repeated. "You can either cease your efforts to drive them bonkers, or I can feed you to the hungry dragon as a midafternoon snack. What's it going to be?"

"We can also turn you over to the police," Jameson added, giving me a no-nonsense look.

The Coblynau darted a glance at the toothy grin of the dragon and shut his mouth, turning his glare on me. "Where am I supposed to go?"

"Seriously? It's a large planet. You can find yourself some hole to crawl in that is far away from here." I shook my arm to add emphasis to my words. "As you've seen, we can find you. If you remain here, I'll bring salt and pepper with me next time to season you before handing you over."

Gethin huffed, drooled, and darted his pointed tongue out to drive the point home. He brought his snout right up to the Coblynau's face and narrowed his eyes.

"The dragon said that includes leaving anyone else that carries my father's blood alone," Rhiannon stated, crossing her arms in anger.

Pixies were so cute when they tried to be scary. "Do we have an understanding?" I shook the Coblynau again.

If looks could kill, I'd be a goner. "Can you give me a ride to the town borders?" he asked me with a snarl.

I called on my magic to bound the vindictive creature up even tighter. "Sure. I'm not carrying you back to my vehicle, though. You'll have to play nice with the dragon."

Rhiannon doubled over and laughed when the Coblynau urinated all over himself when Gethin plucked him from my hold, his teeth puncturing the clothes the Coblynau wore. It felt like poetic justice but smelled awful.

"What did you eat, a ton of rotten asparagus?" I fanned my hand in front of my face. "Sorry, Gethin."

The dragon took to the air in a mighty whoosh of flapping wings with the evil little Coblynau dangling from his mouth. A sight I would cherish for a while.

Rhiannon, Jameson, and I walked back to the stone

palace, where Rhiannon paid me in full and promised that I could return to work with Gethin on improving the use of my magic. It was an enticing offer, and I wondered if I could get another ride on his back while he growled. That part I liked.

Jameson and I set off to the Jeep, where we found an extremely unhappy Coblynau waiting for his ride out of town. After dropping Jameson off, I drove straight to Mick's bar, which straddled the border of Glimmering Rock and Branstone, the human city.

Mick himself was perched outside the door as if he knew I was approaching. I ignored the look he gave me and hauled out the Coblynau. "This little shit is to leave town and not return, or he becomes dragon food," I informed the alpha shifter.

"Remove your bindings, and we'll ensure he is gone," Mick motioned to a couple of wolves lounging around. "I'll be by later so we can have that talk you promised."

Well, damn. At least Rhiannon would sleep tonight.

Book 9
Cakewalk

Chapter One

Here I am, Risa Sanders, P.I. extraordinaire—and I say that with accuracy, not ego—I digress, here I am, running. I'm not a runner. If you see me running, that means you should probably run too in most instances, that is. However, this time, I was running to burn off excess energy to get my mind off the town's alpha wolf, Mick, who was making my life uncomfortable.

Though, I guess if I wanted him to leave me alone, all he would need to do is see me right at this moment. Sweaty, red-faced, huffing and puffing for precious oxygen, and my arms flapping like a deranged bird that forgot how to fly. Let's not forget my feet slapping on the pavement in ten-year-old sneakers like I was a herd of elephants that saw a killer mouse, and my boobs flopping and flapping in the sorry excuse for a sports bra that I bought for its cuteness, not functionality. Lesson learned. All in all, it was a hideous sight that no one could find attractive.

The effort was wasted since my libido hadn't changed in the least. If anything, the subconscious part of my mind was working overtime on picturing the overbearing wolf-man in various scenarios that left the parts of my body not running, sweatier than they should be. All in the name of trying not to think about how much farther I had to run to make it back to my ride home.

I began to slow down to round the corner. I could visualize my feet going in the opposite direction of my body and my face kissing the pavement. That would be right in time for Mick to pop up somewhere and witness the whole thing with my luck. Only, that's not what happened.

A garden gnome came flying through the air with a streak of fire coming off its rear and shattered on the sidewalk in front of me, causing me to windmill my arms to keep my feet under me and hope none of the gnome shards speeding through the air cut me up. *What in the world?!*

I bent over and braced my hands against my knees, and tried to catch my breath. My eyes became glued on the flaming butt of the broken gnome. I shook my head and blinked the sweat dripping off my eyelashes away. Who knew that eyelashes could sweat?

Once I was sure I wasn't going to pitch forward in pure exhaustion, I righted myself and got a Charlie horse in my calf that had me cursing and trying to walk it out. In my three hundred plus years of existence, I had no clue why I thought exercise would work. Worst idea ever, because now I needed to get my pathetic self back to my office where my Jeep waited for me.

I glanced around me, looking for more projectile gnomes, and then started to move again, but not at a run, more of a brisk walk. I made it fifteen feet when a female voice halted me.

"Excuse me! Hello, there! Excuse me!"

"Uh, hello?" I turned in a circle looking for the owner of the voice. My only assumption was that they were behind the considerable barrier of tall hedge-like trees. Super tall, come to think of it. Whoever launched that gnome over those had some serious intentions.

"Sorry if that hit you! I didn't know anyone was out

there!" the stranger's voice called out again. "Hope you are okay. I'm late for an appointment, or I'd take the time to check on you."

"I'm fine," I answered and glanced at my watch. If I didn't hustle, I'd be late too. Guess that meant I was going to be running again. I sighed and started to jog. Three steps later, I tripped over a piece of broken gnome and pitched forward into warm muscular arms that were beginning to be way too familiar.

"Walking long?" Mick drawled, pushing me back to standing.

"If you are keeping track, that was called running," huffed back in irritation.

"Oh, I know. I was watching you," Mick winked, and to his credit, his eyes didn't wander to my chest, which knew was soaked in sweat and had erect nipples pointing right at him.

"Are you following me?" Damn the man. "Because you know, that's considered stalking."

"You wish," Mick chuckled. "You're under my skin, but you aren't that good, Risa. I was in the neighborhood checking on one of my pack. She's about to give birth, and as you know, there's a shortage of cubs. I want to make sure she's good. What the hell are you doing out here anyway?"

"Running," I scoffed at him and made the mistake of gesturing at my exercise clothes.

His eyes roamed freely over my body, and a slow smile spread across his face. "That wasn't running. I don't know what you call it, but regardless, it was fun to watch." His infuriating smile almost made me drool. Mick placed his hand on the center of my back. "Just the way I like you, nice and wet."

I spluttered and almost tripped again. Why did I let Mick get to me like this? "You're a dog." I couldn't think of anything else to say.

"Wolf, but close. Interesting shade of red hair there, Risa," Mick's tone changed to husky when he said my name.

I silently cursed this newly bloomed magic that left my emotions on display for everyone to witness. "Red is angry," I huffed in irritation.

"It's also passion," Mick pointed out insolently. He tapped his nose when I glared at him. "I can smell the pheromones."

"Ugh! I hate you sometimes!" I blurted out for lack of anything else constructive to say.

"That's a lie. I can smell those too." Mick pushed me to the side and pressed me against the tree, his body a scant few inches from mine. He bent and breathed me in, and a low growl trembled in the space between us. "My wolf wants me to mark you."

The words were low-pitched, and it took me a moment while they sunk in for me to process that statement. Wolves mate for life. That one sentence scared me worse than anything else ever had. I wanted to shove him away from me, yet I was terrified to touch him because I knew, without a doubt, my body would betray me. I took the cowardly way out and stood utterly still and said nothing.

Mick finally backed away from me, his eyes rapidly flashing between his normal human eyes and his wolf eyes. He put a few more feet of space between us and frowned. "You never have to be scared of me, Risa. Let me drive you wherever you need to go."

"I'm not afraid of anyone." Indignation rose quickly at his comment.

Mick merely tapped his nose again and walked briskly to his truck. "Get in. I got shit to do."

This banter was more familiar territory for us. I

152

wanted to argue, but honestly, I was too tired, and now a tad shook by the revelations I don't think he intended to make. Perhaps I moved too slowly for his likes because he reached out and hauled me up into his truck when I was within reaching distance and slammed the door.

Chapter Two

My new prospective client, Kristen, would have to deal with a sweaty me. I was polite enough to change into a clean set of clothes, but there wasn't time to help my hair and face. I yanked my hair back into a ponytail and surveyed the pile of exercise clothes.

With a sigh, I scooped them up and stuffed them into my desk drawer, and wiped my hand on the leg of my pants. I used my foot to push the drawer in and tried to make a mental note not to leave them in there. They were wet enough to mildew in that enclosed space. That wouldn't help the smell any.

I paced around the office and noticed that a shadow must have darkened the sky because the office grew darker. I only briefly thought about it since weather changes happened, even in magical cities. I glanced at my watch, and I saw it was time for Kristen to be here.

I walked back around my desk, pulled a contract from my top drawer, and set it on my desk. A tapping sound at my window had me turning around to look.

My heart plummeted, then skyrocketed when my gaze landed on a fiery half-bird, half-dragon-looking creature that had to dwarf the building in size. Its face, or snout, was pressed against the window, and I automatically backed up to put a little distance between us.

The back of my knees hit my spiteful chair and dropped me into the seat. The chair immediately rebounded and flung me right at the window where my face slammed into the windowpane. I am ashamed to say I squeaked, and so did the oddly beautiful creature, in a human-sounding voice.

"I'm so sorry!" A voice that sounded the same as the one that apologized for the flaming gnome called out.

Something clicked in my head, and my fear calmed. I slowly reached forward and cranked the window slightly to allow sound to travel better. "Are you by any chance, Kristen?"

"I am." I received a slow nod of the massive head that appeared to be getting bigger. "My magic is wearing off. I need to get into the sky."

None of it made sense to me, but I agreed wholeheartedly. "How about I come to meet you at your house. Behind those tall trees, right?"

"Yes!" With a flap of wings that I swear had the building's stone walls bowing, Kristen took to the sky in a fiery iridescent display of color that had my jaw gaping open. She took up the entire sky.

I was in motion almost immediately. I wanted to know what the creature was. What the woman beast needed, and why I had never seen her before in all of my existence. I snatched my keys from the corner of my desk, and in a last-ditch effort of vengeance, I turned and kicked the awful chair hellbent on my destruction into the wall.

I was so distracted that I didn't see my ex-boyfriend Danny standing outside my building until I was out the door and bolting for my Jeep. It registered too late that he was getting into my Jeep as I opened my driver's side door.

"What the ever-loving fuck do you think you are doing?" I snapped out and held my hand out in front of me.

I don't know what I expected to happen, but I went

156

from wildly curious to hellfire angry in less than a second. My magic that lashed out on my behalf petered out in a cloud of colorful dust as it bounced off a shield the mighty warlock deployed at the last second.

"I just want to talk, Risa," Danny replied coolly. "No need for hostilities."

"You cheated on me and expected me to be okay with it," I fired back. "I don't want to hear about how you tripped and landed with your penis out into some other ho's vagina. It doesn't work that way."

"I was drugged," Danny shot back angrily. "I was also under a spell. I wouldn't voluntarily cheat."

"I'm on a case." That gave me pause, but it wasn't enough to sway my opinion on the matter. At least not now that I was on my way to meet a new client. "I don't have time for this right now."

"I believe the lady said she was busy," Mick's voice startled me.

"Mick, I can handle this." I sighed. I found myself in the middle of testosterone-Ville.

Danny looked over his shoulder at the barely restrained alpha and rolled his eyes. However, the threat worked since he got out of my Jeep. Only, it gave the overbearing wolf an opening for him to put himself in my Jeep with me instead of Danny.

How I went from having no one in my life to having two men having a passive-aggressive pissing match over me, I had no clue. It was confusing and irritating, not to mention unwanted. Was it so wrong to want a satisfying and peaceful sex life?

"We need to talk," Mick growled as he shut the door in Danny's face.

"Can't we do it later?" I half-whined. "I've got a client to meet."

"That's what I need to talk to you about." Mick

157

crossed his arms over his well-defined pecs and smirked at me when he saw I was checking him out. "I dare you, lick me," Mick taunted.

In answer—because honestly, I was about to take him up on that dare—I started my Jeep and pulled out of the parking lot.

Chapter Three

Your client is a Minokawa," Mick told me when I stopped at the stoplight. The expression on his face said that I should know what he meant.

"And?" I widened my eyes and gave him a questioning look.

"She's in hiding. The only people who knew she lived in Glimmering Rock were council members. Something has to have spooked her for her to show herself the way she did today," Mick elaborated. "It's more than a little concerning to me."

My brain started to whine and click as the gears turned. "Explain a Minokawa."

Mick's jaw clenched, and my nether regions tightened in response. Why I found that so utterly sexy was baffling because it meant he was irritated. It also escalated the sexual tension that already thickened the air in the confined space of the Jeep.

Mick raked his gaze over me in a way that made me want to forget all about Kristen. Visions of tying him up and doing what I wanted to him filled my mind with such intensity that I almost drove off the road.

"Whatever you are thinking, go with it," Mick said huskily. "I'm willing and ready."

I let loose a string of curse words that would put a

drunken sailor that moonlighted as a truck driver to shame. "Focus. Not on me. What exactly is a Minokawa?"

"Half-bird, half-dragon. This creature is extremely rare, and for a good reason. It has feathers instead of scales for armor, but they are hard like scales on a dragon. They are also knife sharp and deadly. They have existed for millennia, but not here on this planet. As you saw, their size is prohibitive; a Minokawa is so massive that it can swallow the sun. That was its purpose back in the early times. Swallow the sun; an eclipse is how it would be seen here, plunge the earth into darkness, descend and kill off the human race," Mick explained in a terrifying monotone.

"How exactly did one end up here in a city on the planet it wants to destroy?" I asked in disbelief, trying to mask the squeaking sound in my voice.

"Kristen isn't a typical Minokawa. Did she appear threatening to you?" Mick cajoled me.

"No," I admitted. "Still doesn't explain how something big enough to swallow a sun ended up here on a planet that is a lot smaller than the sun."

"The last I heard is there are three Minokawa in existence. Two males and Kristen." Mick's expression told me more than the sentence he verbalized did.

"She's supposed to produce a child," I guessed. "Can you imagine the size of the dick on one of those?" I blurted out. I wasn't sorry about it either.

Mick blinked slowly. "Not something I care to ponder. Regardless, Kristen was about half the size of a normal female, making her easy prey for the males. She's still considered quite young for her race, and she isn't ready to produce a child. Kristen sought sanctuary through an unnamed source and wound up here. There is some mighty powerful magic at play to make it so she can remain here. Her property, beyond those trees you were next to, is shrouded in magic."

160

Mick's appearance suddenly made sense to me. "I'm going to walk into a pocket dimension, aren't I?" My magic was wonky before I hit this coming into the magical age period of my centuries-old existence. Walking into another world could have consequences for Kristen and me.

Mick's somber nod spoke volumes. "It messes with your sensory abilities. At least it does mine. Space seems to stretch there, and big things here are suddenly small. It's magic created by masters. It defies all logic."

I laughed at that because I defied all logic. Nothing my magic did made sense, and more often than not, it was uncontrollable. It felt like my body was just a house for this self-thinking magic that was supposed to be a part of my genetic makeup.

I pulled onto the street I ran on not too long ago and parked on the road. "Do I just push through the trees?" I wondered. "Wait. Were you really checking on a pack member earlier, or were you checking on Kristen?"

"I wouldn't be here spilling town secrets if I knew what was bothering her or that she was even bothered. I saw her leave your building. She's kind of hard to miss," Mick pointed out. "Senna is pregnant and due any day. I truly was checking on her."

Mick opened the door and climbed out of the Jeep and stretched. His shirt rode up over the waistband of his jeans, and my eyes followed the happy trail of fine hair that disappeared under the well-worn denim. I wasn't ever aware that I licked my lips until yellow eyes were in front of my face, focused on them.

"Don't push my wolf," Mick warned, and my panties melted. "I can barely restrain him."

I wanted to hate this man. I desperately craved the anger that would make me ignore him, yet I was insanely drawn to him and couldn't help taunting him in ways I knew I shouldn't. "Maybe you shouldn't then."

I have never seen him shift so quickly or clothes shred quite that explosively. Had I known his wolf was that close to the surface, I might not have been so mouthy. Oh, who was I kidding? I know damn well that wouldn't have changed my response. Mick was a danger I couldn't help flirting with constantly.

Mick shoved his nose into my crotch and growled. "No doggy style today," I patted the wolf on his head. "I'm late for an appointment."

I turned and followed the line of trees around the corner until I found an opening with a gate and pushed through it. I heard Mick huff somewhere behind me, and I knew that this little episode with him was far from over. Shamelessly, I also knew it was entirely my fault.

Chapter Four

H ello? Kristen?" I called out, feeling the heavy magic in the air wash over my skin. Mick hadn't been exaggerating. It was an oppressive feeling.

The scene in front of my eyes suddenly changed to a house. I didn't know if I felt bigger or it was a trick of magic, but Kristen appeared to be my size. The cozy-looking home was only a little larger than mine, but her gardens were lush and colorful, with blooms everywhere.

Throughout the expansive gardens were spiteful-looking garden gnome statues that looked like they were mocking you. It was an interesting choice of décor but to each their own. I thought little windmill things would be cuter. Hell, even a rusty weather vane would look more inviting.

"Hello," Kristen called out warily. "I'm Kristen. Welcome to my home. We can talk inside."

"I'm Risa." I shrugged. "We can talk wherever you want to. Your flowers are beautiful. You are quite a skilled gardener."

Kristen shuddered, and her feathers all ruffled with a clinking sound, the iridescent sheen of them flaring a bright red before returning to normal. I was more than surprised to see a few feathers fall to the ground. When Kristen stepped on them, and they went right through her foot, I winced. That had to hurt.

"Are you okay?" I tentatively asked.

"I'm used to it," Kristen replied. "Graceful I am not. It hurts, but I heal quickly. Might not be good for you to step on them, though."

I skirted the sharp feathers, followed Kristen inside to see her trip over the leg of her chair and fall into the counter. My eyebrows raised as she righted herself and plopped down onto a stool, only promptly to fall off of it. I began to wonder if she was cursed, and that was why she needed my help.

"Don't mind me," Kristen told me as she stood. "I'm the worst klutz."

Holy wow. Was this behavior typical for Kristen? She was worse than Jonielle, the purple people eater I met a few months back. I had no idea how to respond to that, so I kept my mouth shut for fear of sharp feathers impaling me.

"I'm going to cut right to the point," Kristen stated. "I'm terrified of garden gnomes. Absolutely petrified, and someone keeps putting them in my prized flower beds. All those flowers are edible, and I use them to decorate my cakes. With them out there, I can't gather the flowers I need to fulfill orders."

I stared at Kristen as I absorbed her words. "You are a baker?" Of all the questions to ask, my mind had settled on that one.

"Cake decorator," Kristen corrected me. "Technically, I guess you can call me a baker since I bake the cakes. Decorating is my specialty, though."

My mind wandered, and I wondered how many cakes she had dropped or fallen into in her time here. I didn't think it wise to ask, and to my utter shock, the question remained inside my head instead of falling out of my lips. I couldn't picture this ginormous creature doing the small detail work needed on wedding cakes. Or any cake.

"Okay. Do you have any ideas on who could be doing this? An unhappy customer?" I tossed out the question and focused on the fear of the garden gnomes and their mysterious appearance in her yard. Though I had to admit, I wanted cake now.

"I've never had an unhappy customer," Kristen stated plainly. "It's cake. Who's unhappy with cake?"

"I'm unhappy that I don't have any," I mumbled and tried to gather my thoughts. "True," I conceded, louder. "Any known enemies or competitors that want you off your game?"

Kristen thought longer about this one and shook her head in answer. "My closest competitor makes traditional cakes, where I use edible flowers. Her customers are the ones that don't have much imagination; I'm sorry to say. My customers are eccentric and willing to try new things. There isn't a lot of crossovers."

I drummed my fingers on the table as I thought about reasons someone would want to terrify Kristen in the unusual way they were. "Has anything out of the ordinary happened other than the gnome thing?"

"Oh!" Kristen shot to her feet and hurried out of the room without another comment.

I sat there flabbergasted until I heard the sound of something breaking and shattering on the floor. I jumped up and started to follow after her to investigate.

"I'm okay!" Kristen called from somewhere down the hallway. The statement finished with some grunting sounds and a painful sounding oomph.

I wasn't sure what to do or if she needed help. She came across as independent, and I didn't want to overstep any boundaries. So I stood there helplessly until I saw her coming back down the hallway clutching a paper in her hand. Kristen shoved her arms forward, and her elbow

165

cracked against a wall sconce and shattered the little flame-shaped lightbulb that was in there.

Tiny shards flew through the air and landed on the floor with a tinkling sound. None hit me, but one little piece remained embedded in Kristen's elbow, stuck right between two deadly feathers. Kristen hadn't exaggerated one iota. In the short time I'd been here, she'd tripped, fallen off a chair, I'm not even sure what happened down the hallway, and now the elbow. Impressive.

"Is there something I can do to help you?" I felt terrible and knew that had to hurt.

"I'll be fine." Kristen struggled to get the piece of glass out, and it was driving me crazy.

"Hold still," I commanded and reached out and plucked the glass from her skin, doing my best to avoid the razor-sharp feathers.

"Thanks." Kristen let out a sigh. "Sadly, this is the norm. I swear the only time nothing happens to me is when I sit still and decorate a cake. Anyway, that paper showed up in my mailbox—no envelope or anything, just a piece of paper. I found it odd since only people with strong magic can sense something here, which is why the garden gnome thing is bothersome. How can someone get on my property without feeling like they are getting crushed?"

I furrowed my brow and looked down at the paper I'd forgotten I held. "The torment will never end unless I get what I want," I read out loud. Someone had glued the letters they'd cut out onto the paper like it was some TV show ransom note.

"Is this for real?" I waved the offending paper around in the air. "It seems childish."

"No shit." Kristen nodded emphatically. "It's not exactly public knowledge that those horrific things scare me. Or that I am even here!"

That was what concerned me the most. I gnawed on

my lip as my mind raced through the possibilities, and I kept landing on the same one—Wiley. Glimmering Rock's newest resident, and one proven to be untrustworthy and despicable.

Mick had warned me a while back that he thought someone on the council was in Wiley's pocket. If he were right, that would explain Wiley knowing about Kristen. Hell, I'm an investigator, and I didn't know about her, and I know a *lot* of the town's dirty secrets.

"Do you ever leave the property?" In my mind, I was already cursing at myself for the dumb question I finally asked Kristen. She'd gone out to come to meet me. She also had a cake decorating business.

"I do, though it is rare," Kristen confirmed. "But it's not like I go far, and I usually use a potent spell that disguises me as human. It has a short life span, but it gives me about thirty minutes. I have a shrinking spell and invisibility one that I use to fly wherever I need to go. I use the disguise spell, land, get what I need, and then take off for home. I've only been out twice in the past year. Both times were to the nursery when I had a couple of plants die unexpectedly."

I thought about it for a few minutes. It seemed unlikely that Wiley would be at a nursery, but it wasn't impossible. "What do people see when you use the shrinking spell?"

"From a distance, I'd think they'd only see a bird-like creature about the size of a siren, or a wyvern maybe." Kristen shrugged.

She had arms, but you wouldn't see them unless you seriously looked. They blended with her wings. Wiley might have seen her in the air and followed to investigate since he did black market trading of rare creatures.

"If I brought back a picture for you to look at, would you remember if you'd seen that person?" I wondered. I

167

needed to get a picture of Wiley.

"I could try," Kristen agreed. "Does that mean you'll help me?"

"Of course." I snorted. That was a foregone conclusion the moment Mick had let me in on the secret. I pulled a contract out and set it on the table for her.

"Great. Before you leave, can you get those gnomes out of here?" Kristen asked, reaching for a pen.

Chapter Five

I need a picture of Wiley," I demanded of Mick once was back in my Jeep. I knew the wolf was going to be waiting for me.

In response, Mick stuck his cold, wet nose against my neck and grazed my skin with some seriously sharp teeth. That was new for him, and I held extremely still. Getting bit by a wolf shifter wasn't high on my list of things to get done for the day.

"I'll take that as a yes," I decided for him. "I'll drop you at the bar. I need to run home and pick up some equipment. I'll swing back by on my way back to Kristen's and get the picture from you. Better yet, can you text it? That will save me a trip."

Mick's actions with me today had me rattled, and I didn't want him to know it, though he probably did because of the damn wolf nose smelling thing. Regardless, I kept blabbering about garden gnomes until I pulled into the bar parking lot. Yellow eyes stared back at me as I rambled.

I reached across and pushed the door open for Mick to get out. He gave me a long look, then jumped down out of the Jeep and nudged the door closed. I wasted no time in getting the hell away from the wolf-man and his intense stares.

I made it home in record time and hopped out to get inside. I had some tripwires somewhere, and I was anxious to get them set up around the perimeter of Kristen's ingress points. There couldn't be that many. I grabbed a couple of trail cameras while I was at it. Any motion would trigger them to record, and a video of Wiley breaking the law would be very helpful in getting the council to oust the slimeball.

I was beginning to think of Wiley as my archnemesis. He suited the role well, and there was no doubt in my mind that he had zero good intentions. I was sure of one thing at least, Mick was in my corner on this, and he'd witnessed it for himself. I was also reasonably sure that Wiley played a part in the disappearance of a young female wolf that I'd found not too long ago. I had yet to put that one together, though.

I grabbed a sweatshirt and a sleeping bag in case I needed to stay the night on Kristen's property and then grabbed some protein bars for snacks. I quickly made a coffee in my travel mug and set back out.

What would Wiley gain from making Kristen swallow the sun? If the earth got destroyed, he'd lose a cash cow for whatever illegal operations he had running here. That was the part that I was having a hard time figuring out.

I mean, aside from picturing something able to swallow the sun and its however many degrees of heat it contained. Kristen would need a stomach made of something more robust than steel. It also didn't compute that she was half the size of other Minokawa's. However, I did like the feeling of being tiny in comparison. Who said I had self-image issues? They lied.

I checked my phone for any messages from Mick and frowned when I saw there was still nothing. I honestly didn't want to have to go back to the bar. That was decidedly his turf and put me at a distinct disadvantage.

I groaned in frustration and turned in the direction of the bar. I'd do it in the name of working on a case. It at least gave me a reason to be there and not just another woman going to try to get in Mick's pants. I was firmly trying *not* to do that.

As I was about to pull into the parking lot, my phone dinged with an incoming message from Mick, so I kept going towards Kristen's house instead of stopping. A slow smile spread across my face when a clear picture of Wiley appeared on my screen. Mick had come through for me.

I kept going to drive to Kristen's and parked on the street like I did last time. It was strange how I didn't pick up on any of that magic out here, only when I got close to the trees. Whoever was behind that was incredible and controlled.

I grabbed my stuff from the Jeep and made my way back to where I had entered last time. My brain wandered to what it must feel like to be bigger than a planet and have to use some serious magic to be able to live on the planet you are supposed to destroy. The universe had a screwed-up way of dealing its cards.

Kristen's existence led to many questions, not to mention her way of life. Regardless, I admired the woman and hoped that I'd be able to help her bring down Wiley. My gut told me he was involved, and I aimed to prove it. If Wiley hadn't made things personal, I'd have just let my feelings toward him go and avoided him. I couldn't now; he'd pursued me and taunted me more than once.

I turned and set one of the cameras in the tree so the sight would be the entrance, and anything that crossed it would get seen. Did I mention that these cameras weren't regular trail cameras? They picked up magical essences too. I'd had them specially made for me. The camera would blend with the tree's branches without

171

impeding the view.

Satisfied, I entered and carefully closed the gate behind me. I turned and about shit myself when I saw Kristen in the air. She was a magnificent beast. The fear of gnomes didn't make sense to me, given her terrifying size, and it made the fact that she could decorate elaborate cakes even more impressive. She just needed to step on whoever was messing with her; she didn't need me. Regardless, Kristen hired me to do a job, and I was going to do it.

I had to applaud the mastery of magic that created this space to make Kristen a home. For a creature that was large enough to swallow the sun, the sky she soared around in wasn't blocked by her body. She was a magnificently mammoth beast, but I still saw blue sky around her. I experienced a moment of pure envy.

In my seconds of staring at Kristen in admiration, I saw her look down and nod her head at me in acknowledgment that I was there. Seconds later, the beastie tripped while flying. I've never seen anything like that happen before in all my years.

One moment Kristen soared through the air with grace and ease, then the next second, she passed through a cloud, and it was like it concealed a tripwire. Kristen suddenly was tumbling through the air with her knife-like feathers flinging all about and landing tip down in the earth like precise weapons.

I yelped when one sliced through my hair, and a yellow lock fell at my feet. It was too close for comfort, and I leaped backward out of reflex and tripped over a feather. Simultaneously, Kristen landed with a shriek and a wild flap of wings that tossed me like a ragdoll. When did it become midnight?

172

Chapter Six

Risa?" Kristen's voice jarred me into consciousness. "Can you sit up? Want a piece of cake?"

"Did you just offer me cake?" I struggled to push myself up to a sitting position. I needed to reevaluate my priorities if cake would make me push past whatever injury I sustained.

Kristen laughed, and I fell a little in love with her at that point. "I did. A girl's gotta do what works to get the desired results. Hold still a second, and then we'll have some cake."

To my utter shock, she jabbed a feather into her hand and dripped some blood on my leg that had a feather impaled through it. When did that happen? Crap. Did I pass out again? "Where's the cake?"

Kristen yanked the offending feather from my leg and tossed it off to the side. "Inside. Don't move yet. Let the blood do its work. There are healing benefits to my blood that will help close this up." Kristen stood up, once again looking a somewhat average size.

Maybe I'd lost a lot of blood or something. My leg was tingly and numb-like, and it felt like a dead weight attached to my hip. I tried to push myself to my feet and instead fell right over and bowled Kristen over—it was a circus act between the two of us.

"Is it normal that I can't feel my leg?" I rolled off of Kristen.

"Hell if I know; I'm not a doctor." Kristen sat up and rubbed the back of her head. "What did I hit?"

Kristen reeled backward and tripped over me since I still sat on the ground with a dead leg. She swiveled around on her butt and shrieked in fear. I leaned forward to see what had freaked her out and did my best to silence the chuckle that built up inside.

Kristen's head had smashed against a garden gnome, and the face was still intact, staring up in accusation. It was too much. I used the leg I could feel and brought my heel down on it, and obliterated the ceramic face into dust.

"All good. Gnome's dead," I called out cheerily to Kristen, who was still trying unsuccessfully to back away. I scooped up the large pieces that remained and dumped them in the bucket off to my side. "Was this here when you took flight? I thought I'd gotten them all earlier."

Kristen stammered out some nonsense before she finally got to her feet and raced to the house. I scooted over to a tree and used it as leverage to get to my feet. My ultimate goal was to get into the house where the promised cake waited for me. I took a moment to look around because I was sure I had picked all the stupid gnomes up from her yard.

I spied a couple more and shook my head in irritation. It seemed almost strategic, but whoever placed them wouldn't know that Kristen would trip over a cloud while flying. Or would they? What kind of luck was that to land on something that scared the life out of you?

The burning sensation of feeling crept back into my dead limb, and I tested it by adding weight to that leg to see if it would buckle. It held even if it wobbled a bit. I decided that the tree I'd leaned against was a good place for another of the cameras, and I got to work setting it up. The camera blended with the tree perfectly. The corner of my mouth twisted up in a half-smile.

Happy with the view the camera would provide, I took careful steps to Kristen's house and tapped on the doorframe. When Kristen didn't respond, I did it again, a little louder this time—still nothing.

"Hello? Kristen?" I called out as loud as I could without yelling.

Something crashed from the back of the house, which I now understood was usual. I waited patiently. Okay, not entirely patiently. After all, there was cake waiting for me somewhere inside that house.

When the sound of things breaking got closer, I announced myself again. "Kristen? Are you in there?"

"Yeah. I'm in here, Risa. Come on inside. I was looking for some pants left here by a friend a while ago. I didn't think you wanted to remain in holey and bloody pants." Kristen tossed a pair of velour baby pink pants at me as she came into view.

I gaped at the pants that had to be from the seventies. I hoped with the way my thighs rubbed together that I wouldn't start a fire. I had to admit that Kristen was right. My pants were already crusty on the outside and sort of sticking to my skin inside.

I peeled the jeans off and hesitantly stepped into the most comfortable pants my ass had ever worn. Also, the ugliest. They were about three inches too short for me, but I didn't care. They were soft, and now they made noise when I walked. Apparently, the pants built some static electricity because when I walked into the kitchen and touched the fork, I zapped myself.

"Your hair is interesting," Kristen commented as she

175

pulled out a beautifully decorated cake that made me think of a tropical island with all the flowers that graced the top of it in pinks, orange, and purple. "It matches the theme of the cake. It was for a job I had won, but they canceled at the last minute."

I was a child. I wanted to dip my fingers in the delectable-looking frosting and taste it. I might have even drooled. "What kind of cake is it?" I reached out and took the cake from the Minokawa so she didn't drop it and I wouldn't get a taste. Purely selfish reasons.

"We are going to skip over the color-changing hair?" Kristen cocked her head to the side. She turned to grab some plates. "The cake is a vanilla lavender. That's what they requested."

I hummed an appreciative sound. I'd never tried a lavender cake, but it smelled like it would make me happy. I was down to try new things. I was salivating before the plate hit the table in front of me.

"My hair is a mystery. It likes to change color with my moods. It's a recent development when the magic I thought I never had decided to settle in and make itself known. It's inconvenient, to say the least, but I think it will save me in the long run from having to color it," I informed Kristen. "Tell me a little about you while we devour this delicious concoction."

"Well, let's see. Before I came here, I was out in the vast space of the universe. You know, where I can be me without living inside a magic bubble to disguise me. I've known the legends about our existence since I was old enough to understand. It didn't sit right with me that we were supposed to destroy this place. The two males that were out there with me thought I was a misguided female." Kristen shook her head in disgust and cut a wedge out of the cake, plopped it onto a plate and slid it across the table to me.

"Sounds like a chauvinistic pig," I declared. It would be rude to smash my face into the cake and eat it without a fork, wouldn't it?

"They pursued me with no holds barred. It's a who has a bigger tool, can make it dance better, and piss farther game. I wanted nothing to do with it. I hate their attitudes and superiority complexes. I told myself there was something better out there for me than them. I sought out some of the ancient masters and begged for spells that would allow me to enter the earth," Kristen told me as she cut her piece of cake.

"I don't blame you," I said with a mouthful of the cake. "Men are pigs. Across all races."

Kristen snickered at me as I stuffed my face. "I guess you like the cake."

I nodded because my mouth was too full to speak without spitting food everywhere, and this cake was not to be wasted. I supposed that my actions spoke louder than any words I could think to say. Because, seriously, I wasn't going to slow down on feeding my face. I had energy to regain after my feather impaling.

"One of the elders from the town's council found me in a remote section of the Sahara and brought me here. He swore the others to secrecy, and they blended their magic to create this space for me. It's ingenious magic, and it works for me. It stretches to suit my needs and has absolutely no scientific logic. I don't understand it at all, but I'm grateful for it," Kristen went on.

I finished my last bite of cake and gave a pathetic look at the remaining dessert. Shaking myself out of it, I turned my head to face Kristen. "I can't imagine. It must be lonely."

Kristen shrugged. "I do alright. I have customers and a few friends who stop by to visit me. Mick stops by too. The creators come once a year to reinforce the magic.

177

They do that to make sure the spell doesn't collapse."

That was a horrifying thought I didn't want to ponder. "Okay. Let me show you the cameras I put up. I'm going to hang around out here all night."

Chapter Seven

Given that Kristen's domain was pure magic, the weather was perfect, and I didn't freeze the way I anticipated. I refused to think about the creepy crawlies around me, and I knew they were there. They had to be since they kept the garden going with their insect ways buggy stuff that made my skin itch thinking about it.

I was out of range of the cameras by design. I didn't want any of my movements to set them off inadvertently. I wasn't a fan of being on camera and didn't want to sift through hours of video looking for something captured that wasn't me.

After training with a Red Welsh Dragon named Gethin, I noticed that I could feel my magic up its sensitivity level. Sitting out here in the dark, I could feel when odd ripples of magic traveled through the air.

I found it odd that I could sense the ripples given the heavy pressure of the magic that existed in this pocket space already. It was strange that I adapted to the feeling of being inside here and that my skin wasn't crawling with the urge to escape. I shrugged it off and concentrated.

Every ten minutes or so, I'd hear noises from Kristen inside while she worked on a cake for someone, mumbling words too faint for me to make out. Then, like clockwork every thirty-five minutes, I'd hear a loud crash sound and string of curse words that signified she tripped over something. It amazed me that she didn't drop cakes.

I did my best to concentrate on the ripples until I felt my magic lockdown on the location where they originated. It was not from the gate that I went through. It stemmed from the opposite side, which I assumed was only a bubble of sorts, no actual entrance or exit. Interesting.

I didn't know anything about the perimeter of this space or even understand the magic that created it. I'm not sure Kristen did either. I was also of the mind that with her feather/scales that she would be impervious to any magic thrown her way.

Kristen didn't hire me for protection; I reminded myself. She hired me to find out who was torturing her with garden gnomes. Kristen didn't strike me as the kind to be scared easily by another magical being, given that she could swallow the sun without cooking herself and that, as far as I knew, she was the most enormous creature out there. That alone would intimidate any predators. Well, other than the males that wanted in her pants.

Wait. Could this be an act by one of the males and not Wiley? Were they trying to scare her back out into the open? I couldn't discount the theory, even though I wanted to catch Wiley trying to break the law again. On camera would be ideal so I could stuff it down the throats of the council members. Oops, I got off track.

Another of those ripples washed across my skin. I stood up, my instincts screaming at me to move, so I stepped to the side and became partially obscured by the tree where I had mounted the camera. I stared in the direction my senses told me the magic originated and watched in fascination as a spell moved through the air.

It aimed right where I had hidden, which told me someone other than Kristen knew I was there. The dulling pressure of this space must have affected spell work because it was moving like it was stuck in mud, rolling end over end, and was slow enough that I watched it move and undulate. Even if I had remained in place, I would have had time to get out of the trajected path.

It was an exciting phenomenon to witness. The colors momentarily distracted me from my objective, which was to find out who was behind this dazzling display of slow-motion magic. I grudgingly had to admit that it was mesmerizing.

Shaking myself out of it, I side-stepped again and moved into the shadow of the tree, and knelt. The few times I'd worked with the Red Welsh Dragon Gethin, I'd gotten a better handle on my magic and the things I could do. According to him, I was pretty powerful.

I reached inside for the vibrating pool that I felt in the pit of my belly and let the sensation wash over me. When it felt like it would snap me in half, I released it. It took less time than it usually did, and I formed a clear intention in my mind of what I wanted that power to do.

The brilliant display of magic far outclassed the mildly sparkly spell that meandered toward me. I wanted to pat myself on the back; I was so proud of my work. I might genuinely pat myself if the spell did what it was supposed to do.

I got so caught up in my awesomeness that I ignored the magic creeping towards me. That is until it exploded against the ground like a nuclear bomb and threw me thirty feet into the next clump of trees. I'd like to say it didn't hurt, but it did.

"Motherf—" I started to scream. I got cut off by an unholy screech that made my bladder quiver, and I was grateful for all the extra Kegels.

A very pissed-off Kristen made an appearance. Her feathers were iridescent and deadly as they similarly rose

181

from her body like a porcupine when threatened. I didn't know what the goo was on the end of them, but I knew I didn't want to be on the receiving side of her anger. This woman most assuredly didn't need my protection.

My magic landed with an impact more significant than a nuclear bomb and illuminated the space with a blinding light that changed Kristen's angry screech to a squawk. Perhaps I should not have put so much into it. I couldn't see any better than anyone else could. That meant we were all vulnerable.

Chapter Eight

With heightened senses, I made my way to where Kristen had last been when the lights came on, and I heard a loud oomph. I rapidly blinked and tried to get my eyes to focus while I mentally blasted myself for not thinking of safeguards for the spell.

With lightning-fast thinking skills, I formulated another thought and sent out a surge of magic that again left us stumbling. Well, I stumbled, Kristen flat out fell.

"Who turned out the damned lights?" Kristen yelled in an exasperated tone.

"Sorry," I mumbled. I squinted and tried to get my eyes to adjust faster because that little danger instinct was rapidly growing. I blinked a few times, then squeezed my eyes shut and whispered a little prayer for vision.

I opened them to see Kristen staring at me in confusion. "Your hair is black, purple, and gray."

"Isn't multi-color the trend now?" I fired off as I dove to the ground. "Stay down."

A garden gnome sailed over my head and landed with a thump next to Kristen. The ungodly bellow that came out of that woman's mouth about had my ears bleeding. I clapped my hands over them and elbow crawled over to her to snatch the gnome up before she permanently deafened me.

"Relax!" I yelled. "I've got it." To prove my point, I grabbed a rock near me and smashed the little decorative and harmless statue, and about pissed myself when it came to life. This act in no way calmed Kristen down.

"Stupid bitch!" the gnome cursed at me. "Are you trying to kill me?"

"As a matter of fact, I am." I grabbed the mouthy little bastard by the back of his happy red clothes and stood up, dangling him in front of me. "What are you doing here?"

Kristen began to tremble, and razor-sharp feathers got launched in all directions. He started to flail about like a lunatic when one narrowly missed the not-so-innocent gnome. Kristen's fear was visceral, and I was more than a little concerned for my safety.

"Kristen, go back inside," I ordered her in my best mother tone. "I need to interrogate this little shit. You don't want to see what happens."

Unfortunately, Kristen had managed to get tangled up in the garden hose, and her frantic movements had her good and stuck. Her kicking legs struck one of the pipes the hose connected to, and a spray of water came bursting out in a geyser.

It wasn't like I could put the gnome down and help her, he'd bolt, and I'd lose whatever opportunity I had in trying to find out why he was here and on whose orders.

"What do you mean she isn't going to want to see what happens?" the angry gnome snapped out. He was moving so much I almost lost my grip on him.

"It means your life was forfeit the moment you stepped onto this property." I shook him around. "I'd think really hard about sharing everything you know. It might make me spare your life."

Kristen had taken the opportunity to roll as far away from me and the little creature as she could. She succeeded in wrapping even more of the hose around her. She was the perfect prey at the moment, and I felt something ma - intentioned approaching.

"Kristen, you need to free yourself right now. I've got a hold of this thing. He can't get to you. But whoever sent him can. Snap to it, cake lady."

My words prompted action and a wail. "The cake is destroyed!"

Grief settled deep in my bones at the momentous loss. "Well damn."

It took a few minutes, but Kristen got untangled. "Someone is coming."

I already knew that but wisely chose to keep my mouth shut for once. Kristen's feathers went from the iridescent whites to an orange-red, and she took a deep breath in. It was marvelous, and I was distracted by it. Luckily, the gnome was too.

"Lady, that can't mean anything good. Let me go!" The garden gnome's rosy red cheek circles had lost their cheery color, and his eyes got beady.

"Not a chance. At the very least, I'm turning you over to the police and the council for prosecution and punishment for the crime of trespassing with ill-intent."

"*You* tried to kill *me!*" The gnome's tone turned indignant. "I'm going to press charges against you!"

I laughed. Let the silly man try. My breath caught as a figure materialized, and it wasn't one that I recognized. I narrowed my gaze on him and scented magic that felt familiar to me.

"Drop the glamour!" I shouted as Kristen let loose whatever she'd been doing.

A stream of white fire erupted from her mouth. Only it didn't incinerate everything in its path. It was focused and precise and hit exactly where the figure had been standing. The man was there, and then he was gone. I didn't understand.

"What happened?" I wondered out loud, forgetting about my temporary prisoner who'd gone utterly still.

"It's magic fire." Kristen sighed. "Something similar to short-circuiting electronics, only for magic. He shouldn't have been able to leave via magical channels."

"You two are idiots," the gnome mumbled haughtily.

"Says the moron who got captured and almost brained to death." I tilted my head to glare at the obnoxious little man. "Suffering from little man syndrome, are you?"

Kristen chuckled but kept her distance from us. She scanned her yard, and I guessed she was looking for more gnomes or evidence of someone still out there. Kristen let out an annoyed huff of mostly smoke and turned to head back into the house.

"Don't leave blood splatters. It will taint the soil."

"Of course." I grinned in response and shook my arm again, which was getting tired. I knew there was a reason I liked this woman so much.

Chapter Nine

How many more of you are there tormenting this poor woman?" I demanded in a gruff tone.

I conducted this interview with proper channels and in the Glimmering Rock police station. I didn't have many friends here, but some helpful intervention from the council made it work.

"I've already answered this, you boobed idiot." The gnome glared at me with his mouth screwed up in a snarl. "There is only me. I got hired, and it was done with magic. The same magic got used to project the image that the lady tried to burn. You saw how well that worked."

It seemed more like technology to me than magic. However, I wasn't exactly up to date on all magical abilities, having spent most of my life without them. The officer assisting me had hooked the gnome named Fabio to a lie detector machine. He gave me a slight nod to let me know Fabio told me the truth.

"Who hired you, dickems?" That was my best attempt at getting back at Fabio for the boobed idiot comment.

"I don't know," Fabio sighed dramatically. "It was done through a third party, and I don't even know that guy's name. He looked like the guy who disappeared. I haven't seen him around here before, and he never showed up in person to our meetings. Only the projection."

Another nod from the officer. I had gathered the cameras that had recorded all the action and had copies made that I handed over to the council. I knew without a doubt that Mick would be poring over the footage himself.

"Why?" I asked Fabio.

"He wanted the woman scared out of her space," Fabio shrugged.

The officer shook his head. Fabio had lied.

"Try telling me the truth." I rapidly lost patience with this and felt close to physically harming the asshole.

"I did," Fabio smirked at me. "It just wasn't the whole truth."

The smirk only lasted a few seconds because I shocked him with my magic like a taser. I took great pleasure in watching his little body flop around like a drop of oil on a hot skillet. It left him panting, and the officer did nothing to intervene. In fact, he had a slight smile on his face.

"Police brutality!" Fabio screamed.

It was a soundproof room. I rolled my eyes. "I'm not the police, and I can vouch for the officer over there that he never touched you."

"I can and will testify that Risa never touched you," the cop backed me up. Surprising.

"Fine." Fabio's shoulders drooped. "It wasn't really the female that was the target. My job was to get her so scared she left that place. The theory was her presence would frighten everyone here, and she'd have no choice but to return to space and draw out the males. The males were the targets. Capturing the female was a bonus because they could mate, and the resulting baby would get taken."

My stomach rolled. I knew it was Wiley behind this; only there was still no way to prove it. "Lock him up." I stood and walked out of the room and didn't stop until I sat in my Jeep.

I drove back to my office, wrote a report for Kristen, and stuck it in an envelope with my invoice. I'd drop it off to her and then go home and drink myself stupid.

My head was too filled with images of baby trafficking and forced mating. It was revolting. I don't remember the drive back out to Kristen's. I parked on the street and had barely made it in the gate when I spotted Kristen talking with Mick.

Damn it all. I couldn't catch a break. Brushing off the rising estrogen in my bloodstream, I stalked forward and handed Kristen the envelope as she handed Mick a box.

"Thank you, Risa. It wasn't quite the cakewalk I expected it to be, but you handled it better than I could have hoped. I'll read over this and get your payment sent out." Kristen winked at me and shoved Mick in my direction.

The slow sexy smile that spread across Mick's face did a number on my nerves. He lifted the box's lid, and I saw a beautiful cake sitting inside. I reached my finger out to swipe a bit of the icing, unable to help myself. I was a kid when it came to cake.

Kristen chose that moment to trip into Mick, who fell towards me. I ended up with the cake smashed into my face and across my chest but managed not to fall over.

"Oops." Kristen chuckled and then took off toward her house. She didn't look sorry in the slightest.

"Cakewalk," Mick's eyes turned smoky looking. He bent his head forward and licked the frosting from my neck before sealing his lips to mine in possibly the hottest kiss I have ever had. I felt the possessive growl from his wolf and pried myself away.

"That's good frosting," I croaked weakly.

"The best I've ever had." Mick's eyes locked on my

189

lips. "Fill me in on what happened before I lick the rest of that off you."

Wait. That was an option? Of course, it was. I couldn't let that happen, though. "You ruined my cake."

Mick's laughter followed me to my Jeep. I knew I was running out of time before giving in to the carnal desire that erupted when he was near me. But it wouldn't be today.

Book 10
Lip Service

Chapter One

R isa Sanders! This is the Branstone Police Department! Open your door!" a male voice yelled from my front porch aggressively; it was four in the morning.

"Chill out, asshole," Mick's voice carried through the door to my ears. *What was he doing here?*

I swung open the front door and took a rigid stance with a no-nonsense expression on my face and my hands on my pajama-clad hips. My gaze immediately went to Mick, who had a highly aggravated look, and his eyes were flashing yellow. Not a good sign for someone.

"To what do I owe this intrusive pleasure?" I snapped at the Branstone cop, who clutched a crinkled piece of paper.

"I have a search warrant to search this premise. You are under suspicion of murder." The cop looked slightly scared then.

"Excuse me?" I felt the anger boiling inside, and I guessed my hair changed colors to accentuate that new emotion.

"What did you do now, super-sleuth?" Mick flashed me a nano-second of a smile before his face went stormy again.

"I didn't murder anyone, much less someone from Branstone." I didn't budge from my place inside the door.

Nor did I open it further to invite the cop inside. "You will not enter this house until I have my lawyer present."

"He's on his way," Mick growled. "I'm here representing the town council. Branstone police can't operate in Glimmering Rock. This guy doesn't seem to understand that. Why don't you explain who got murdered, cop?"

I hadn't seen Mick that pissed off in a while. It was usually due to my presence or something I did, which would still be true since there was a cop on my doorstep. I also wondered what lawyer he called since Mick had no idea who my lawyer was unless he called Danny. I sincerely hoped that wasn't the case.

"I don't need to reveal any information about an active investigation," the cop smarted off. He backed up three steps when his eyes landed on Mick.

"I have every right to know what I am getting accused of," I challenged. "If this is regarding one of my cases, that warrant better list explicit areas that would pertain to a client. This house is my residence, not my office."

I moved to shut the door, and the cop lost his mind. He lunged for the door to keep it from closing, then yelped in fear. I glanced back and almost laughed as Mick held the cop in the air from his Branstone Police Department uniform collar.

"You can't leave my sight until the lawyer shows up in case you are going in there to remove or hide evidence," the cop squeaked.

"What is your name?" I demanded. "You haven't even announced yourself. How do I know you are legit?"

"D-detective Pupe," the man stammered, still dangling over my porch steps.

"Poop?" I snorted in a very unladylike manner.

The detective scowled at me, and I motioned Mick

to let him down. Once his feet hit the cement, he straightened his uniform and tried to remove the wedge from between his butt cheeks discreetly. I smirked n response.

"I verified his information," Mick told me flatly. "I also provided an alibi."

My eyebrows raised slightly at that. I wisely said nothing. In all my years as a private investigator for my firm called I S.P.I. I hadn't made all that many friends on the Branstone Police force. There were crossover cases where people from the human city came to Glimmering Rock to hire me. However, most human police had no idea that we were a mixed bag of supernaturals.

If Mick provided an alibi for me, he probably called the pack's lawyer, also a wolf, who played no games and was not someone you wanted to cross. Interesting knowledge to have ahead of time. Especially that Mick was my alibi since he didn't lie.

In the distance, I heard the sound of a motorcycle approaching, the engine roaring in response to the speed the rider was using. I crossed my arms under my boobs and leaned against the door frame. Mick's eyes lowered to examine my jutted-out chest, and he graced me with a sultry smile that set some of my body parts on fire.

The sexual tension between the alpha wolf and myself had heightened to intolerable levels the past couple of months, and while I wanted to take him for a ride, I didn't think it would end well for either of us. I couldn't help but admit that the man-wolf was undeniably doable.

Less than two minutes later, the lawyer appeared, pulling in the driveway on the motorcycle, looking like a complete badass biker, which he was. An unhappy one, too, going by the expression on the man's face.

"Risa, say nothing," Hunter Bruce barked.

"She hasn't," Mick answered, that alpha tone

195

bringing Hunter to heel quickly. Even the detective shifted uncomfortably.

"Hand over the warrant," Hunter demanded, his beefy hand held out to the much smaller cop. Hunter read it over quickly, stepped in front of the detective, blocking him from my view. "Risa, it's legit. He can search, but I will be hovering over him the entire time. He will put it to rights if he makes a mess before leaving. Isn't that right, Detective Pupe?" It wasn't a question.

My eyebrows searched for my hairline once again at the overly aggressive tone. I nodded in response and moved out of the way for Hunter to step inside. He took a quick look around and motioned the detective and Mick to enter.

"Mick, stay with Risa on the couch; neither of you speaks unless you are answering me." Mick bristled at being ordered around and gave a terse nod. He put his hand on the small of my back with his fingers grazing my ass and led me to the couch.

I still had no idea what was happening or who had gotten murdered, and it didn't look like I would find out any time soon. Mick pulled me close when we sat, kept his arm around my waist with his hand possessively on my hip. He stuck his nose in my neck and breathed me, making my lady bits quiver.

"Gage's boyfriend is dead," Mick's super-low whisper reached my ear. "Do not react. Gage is fine and under suspicion as well. Hunter has already been over there and is representing you both. Do not argue with me."

My head bobbed just enough to let Mick know I heard him and understood. The knowledge did nothing to calm my overly excited nerves, which came out in my hair color. Gage was my middle son and probably the most sensitive of the three. For him to have his boyfriend murdered and accused of it would be devastating to him.

"He's okay, Risa," Mick reassured me, his lips playing over my neck in a brazen display. "Gage was at work all night and slept in his office. Video evidence proves it."

The relief I felt caused me to lean into Mick and bend my neck to give him easier access. The man oozed sex appeal like a waterfall in a week-long monsoon. That might even be an understatement, and the infuriating wolf-man knew it. Just because I thought that us together was a bad idea didn't mean I didn't enjoy it.

"You know we can have sex, and it doesn't make you my mate unless I bite you, right?" Mick growled in that low pitch tone that drove me wild. Of course, I knew that.

"That's obvious, or the entire female portion of Glimmering Rock would be your mates," I fired back at him. "I'm pretty sure you are only allowed one. Not a town."

Mick's lips paused the delicious trail across my neck that he was blazing and broke out into laughter.

Chapter Two

A couple of hours later, I was back in my office and calling in every favor I could to find out as much information as I could on the murder of Zhor the satyr, Gage's boyfriend. Satyrs were well known for their sexual antics, and that would be my best guess as to why he got murdered. Money, sex, and power were the top three motives.

I didn't get very far when an old client walked into my office with a sheepish look on his face. Chad was another cop from Branstone that I'd helped when he was getting harassed by imps. Only Chad wasn't quite aware of the magical world existing around him.

I occasionally had clients like that, which made working the cases that typically involved magic somehow trickier to explain to the client when I closed it. There was no written law that said we couldn't share the secret of ourselves, though it was frowned upon mainly because t caused people to panic and jump to conclusions that weren't even remotely true.

"Hi, handsome," I greeted Chad with a smile. "What brings you way out here?"

"I need help. The kind of help that my gut says only you can help with," Chad replied with another odd look.

I raised my eyebrows in question and sat there

silently. It was an old trick. When you remained silent, people became uncomfortable and spilled things they wouldn't ordinarily say to fill the silence.

"You know," Chad sighed and waggled his eyebrows.

"Are you flirting?" I guessed. "Is the help you need getting laid?" I got a laugh from him on that one.

"If I didn't have someone I was seeing, I would say yes. After my last case with you, I figured out that there is an unseen existence that not many of us know about." Chad stood up and looked around as if someone were listening to him. "Do you mind if I lock the door?"

I shrugged in response, intrigued. Chad walked over to the door, opened it, peering into the hallway carefully, then popped his head back inside, closed, and locked the door. He tested it twice before he returned to his chair and faced me.

"I'm talking about magic," Chad whispered. "It's real, right?"

I was surprised but still said nothing. Chad wasn't one of those who believed in what he couldn't see, though, to his credit, some strange stuff had happened during his case that he had seen and could not explain. It wouldn't have taken that much for him to leap to a believer. Still, I didn't confirm and watched him squirm.

"You know I'm a cop. This silence thing is something we do with perpetrators to get them to speak. I know what you are doing." Chad crossed his arms and gave me a blank look.

"What do you know about a murder that happened last night. A man named Zhor?" I asked point-blank.

"Is this a trade-off of information?" Chad fired back at me. "You confirm magic, and I confirm that a murder happened?"

"I already know the murder happened. I got

accused of it." I stifled a laugh.

"You're kidding." Chad dropped his arms and gave me an astonished look.

"Nope." I shook my head. "My middle son was accused too. I just had my house searched. Zhor was my son's boyfriend."

"Wow. Okay. I'm not part of that investigation, but I can poke my nose around and see what I can find to help you out. I find it unlikely that you would kill someone." Chad shook his head. "Let me rephrase that. I don't see you killing someone without good reason or immediate threat."

"Fine," I pursed my lips, unsettled that he didn't see the totally unbalanced part of my brain that would allow me to go off the rails and kill someone. He was right, but he didn't have to ruin my badass reputation by admitting it. "What can I do for you?"

"I think someone put a spell on me," Chad blurted out, his face turning beet red. "There's a backstory there that I don't want to get into because it's humiliating. Is that enough for you to investigate?"

My curiosity was at an all-time high. Chad had been pretty open with me in the last case, which involved sex in outdoor spaces with female clients. What could be more embarrassing than telling a stranger that something had poked you in your naked ass in the throes of ecstasy?

"Can you not get it up or something?" I couldn't help asking. "That's a matter of a pill prescribed by a doctor, not a spell put on you. Are you dating a witch?"

If possible, Chad flushed an even deeper shade of red and dropped his eyes, hanging his head down to his chest. I might implode if he didn't give me more information. However, he *was* someone I considered a friend, so I needed to give him a break.

"Okay. Where do you think this happened? You have to give me a little more information than you think

201

someone put a spell on you. Why do you think it's a spell or involves magic?" I tried, pulling my notebook closer to me.

"I was in an establishment here in Glimmering Rock. It was before I started dating my girlfriend, Rebecca. By the way, she's a lot of fun, and she's a meat-eater like me, forget the vegetables. Anyway, I was in this place that offers companionship, and after I left, uh, things changed for me, and it's not something that would happen without the help of magic. That's all I want to say about that," Chad hedged.

"You went to the cathouse in town?" I blurted out, shocked. "Was it for a case you were working?" Chad wasn't someone who would have to pay for sex.

"No," Chad dropped his eyes again. "I was feeling low and depressed."

Enough said. We all felt that way sometimes, though not everyone went to a cathouse to solve the issue. Whatever, it was his life to lead how he wanted. He'd given me enough information to open and work a case.

"I can work with that." I slid a contract over to him. "I will assume that the resolution will be the spell getting lifted and not just who did it?"

"Preferably," Chad agreed, signing. "I'll keep my finger on the information chain in the murder case as a thank you. If I hear something wild, I'll let you know."

Chapter Three

After Chad left, I set off for Lip Service, the cathouse, or house of ill repute, whatever you want to call it. I knew the owner, Lisa. She was a succubus, and the occupation was perfect for her. I knew that she had selective clientele and that not one person that utilized her services was ever dissatisfied.

A succubus was a type of demon that could utterly seduce any living creature through dreams, making them do things they would never do in waking hours. When Lisa turned it on, you were turned on and would do anything to scratch the itch. Lisa is one female no one should mess with, and she ran a tight ship.

Blonde, leggy, stacked, and a smile as sweet as could be, Lisa's charms were apparent. It's what you don't see that gets you. Sharp wit, forked tongue, literally—and I've heard stories about what it could do—and demon powers that even I didn't understand.

I hesitated only a moment before walking into her establishment. I wasn't on bad terms with Lisa; however, she was fiercely loyal to her employees, and I wasn't sure how she would react to me accusing one of them of putting a spell on a client.

"Well, hello there, Risa. I'm surprised to see you here with that hot wolf after your sweet ass. Thanks to you, he hasn't needed services in a while," Lisa drawled. There were barbs in there, but I refused to act on them. Lisa could turn me into a pile of horny goo in about two seconds flat.

"Too bad for him," I replied with a smug tone. "I only need to speak to you."

"You and everyone else today," Lisa huffed. She crossed her arms under her chest, and damn it, I looked. "Zhor's murder is putting a damper on my business with all the cops in and out of here."

"What?" That stopped me in my tracks. "Why were they here?"

"Honey, Zhor worked for me. You didn't know that?" Lisa's eyebrows raised. "Then why are you here?"

"I wanted to ask you a question about a case I'm working on; now that I know about Zhor, I have several more. Not in an official capacity for those." I stared blankly at the sultry succubus for a few seconds. "I have a question about your employees."

"Oh?" Lisa's eyebrows went from raised to one cocked. "Let's hear it." She motioned me to follow her to her office. I sat when she pointed to a chair.

"Do any of your people have the ability to cast spells or curses? Or do you employ any witches, wizards, or sorcerers?" I blurted out.

I could feel her magic working on me, and I fought the urge to shift in my chair. Several parts of my body had a steady rush of blood flowing to them. I had a feeling that any friction in my clothed areas would be my undoing.

"Your strength has grown, my friend," Lisa laughed delightedly. "I'll stop. I appreciate that you didn't walk in here, accuse one of my pets, and instead asked about their abilities. I know you wouldn't be here if something didn't lead you here. That said, I'll talk, no witches on staff or any of the others. Some of them use charms in their services, and all have protective charms. That isn't what you mean, though, is it?"

"No." I shook my head and wondered how to word Chad's complaint without much detail. "My client was here; he didn't give me an exact date. After he left, he started noticing something unnatural happening in a sensitive area," I paraphrased.

Lisa frowned and looked at the ceiling, deep in thought. She perched on the edge of her desk and tapped her heeled toe. I had no idea how she could wear shoes like that, but I had to admit, they accentuated her long legs and nicely rounded butt. Obviously, I was still turned on.

"Wait. I know you can't reveal your client's name, same as me. Was this, by any chance, a human from Branstone that works for law enforcement?" Lisa guessed.

I nodded and wondered how she knew about his profession. It didn't seem like something that Chad would announce unless he were on duty, which we all knew he wasn't. Not that night, though it did lead me to believe that he'd been there before.

Lisa burst out into laughter. She bent forward and smacked her legs as she howled her entertainment loudly. Laughter was contagious, and it wasn't long before I was chuckling right along with her, only I didn't know why and that it was at Chad's expense.

"I can't believe it worked!" Lisa choked out between guffaws.

"What?" I asked, trying to cover my giggles.

"Holy shit. A couple of weeks ago, your client was all depressed and down. I felt it down to my soul, and I asked him if I could be of service. I sincerely wanted him to feel better; that's what my business is all about, right?"

Lisa didn't wait for me to answer, so I nodded my acceptance of the statement. It matched what Chad had told me so far.

"The little fucker looked at me, like up and down, a slow perusal of my goods. I'm not humble, I know what I've got, and I know how to maximize it and use it to my best abilities. I'm not saying I'm a legend, *but I am*. This guy has the balls to say to me, 'You look good, but you're too old for my tastes.' Can you believe that shit?" Lisa stared at me, wanting an answer this time.

"Pretty brazen," I admitted, stifling a laugh. I absolutely could see Chad saying that.

"Since he was a paying customer, I kept my mouth shut because everyone has a type. If he liked younger women, I didn't have a problem with that. I showed him who was available and let him choose. He left happier than when he came in, but he dismissed me again when I tried to conversate with him. So as he was leaving, I cursed with something my grandma did to my grandpa hundreds of years ago when he pissed her off," Lisa explained.

I couldn't wait to hear this. Chad had insulted the wrong woman, that much was clear, and I would have no problems telling him that for future reference.

"Every time the mood strikes, his junk would turn to a vegetable," Lisa declared. "It was quite effective at frustrating my grandpa, and I figured it would be the same this time."

It took me a moment while I went over the conversation with Chad and how he talked about what his girlfriend didn't like to eat, and then I burst out laughing. Rebecca didn't like vegetables. Even if she knew what had happened, she wouldn't be playing in Chad's pants since her tastebuds were for sausages, not green beans.

"Creative, right?" Lisa said proudly. "Should teach that man to treat women with more respect and not insult them to their faces."

No wonder Chad hadn't told me the specifics. I couldn't stop laughing. If he'd said that to me, I would have done something to him, too. I don't know if I would have been colorful enough to think that up on my own, but I would have done something.

Once my laughter died down, I wiped the tears from my face and looked at Lisa. "Is there any chance that you can remove the curse?"

"I could. Why should I? I'll *maybe* consider it if he apologizes to me, and it's sincere. Otherwise, he can grow a garden and make salads from his erections." Lisa huffed in irritation. "I'm so tired of men and their shit."

"Preach it, sister." I held my fist up in solidarity. "They should all be cursed with baby carrots and Brussel sprouts."

Chapter Four

After an hour of insane laughter and jokes at Chad's expense and his new, unused vegetable garden, we finally calmed down.

"Now onto the serious stuff," I began. "What do you know about Zhor and his murder?"

"Honey, I know a lot about that satyr. He was a serial dater, great at his job, and a master manipulator. Relationships with that man didn't last longer than two and a half months. Zhor didn't lie with his words, but his actions spoke differently. He was only one of three males here, and he was popular with everyone across the board. All those myths and legends about satyrs and being sexual were entirely true. Given the right motivation, he could out dirty me, and I'm a succubus. It doesn't surprise me in the least that someone murdered him, though his loss saddens me," Lisa told me.

"Zhor was dating my middle son, Gage. As far as I knew, they'd been together a couple of months, though there have been hints that things weren't as peachy as they could have been. My ex, Danny, dropped a few hints, along with my youngest son," I admitted. "My motives here are purely selfish so that I can keep Gage from being a suspect. Oh, and they also suspect me."

"Why?" Lisa scoffed. "Because you're the

boyfriend's mom? Ridiculous." Lisa waved her hand through the air dismissively. "Your son is the devilishly handsome chef?" Lisa looked more intrigued by that than the topic of her employee's murder.

"Has Gage been here?" I asked while simultaneously nodding to her question.

"No. Zhor talked about him frequently. Oh, and while we're talking, I'd like to hire you to find out what you can about someone that was harassing Zhor. A client, I presume, but I saw blackmail notes where he threatened to expose illegal activity at Lip Service. I want to know why, how, and who," Lisa declared hotly.

Startled by the sudden switch in topic, I could only blink rapidly while my thoughts tried to reform themselves. Blink, blink, blink, pause, what the hell?

"Oh, I'll pay you if you are worried about that." Lisa stared at me intently, waiting for my response. "You have contracts you send, right? I'll write my email address down for you, and you can send it over." She reached for a paper pad on her desk, wrote the address down, and handed it to me.

"Uh, okay." I took the paper from her and slid it into my pocket.

"Fascinating hair," Lisa remarked, her interest piqued. "Is that a charm? It's been changing since you got here."

"Sadly, no." I shook my head. "My magic bloomed late, and it's manifesting in odd ways. Apparently, my hair color matches my mood. I can't get away with shit."

Lisa howled with laughter, doubling over again. "I'm sorry," she gasped out. "I wouldn't be able to keep my business open if my hair did that."

I guess that answered the question of sex workers faking their orgasms. Good to know if I ever wanted to hire one.

"I'll get that contract sent over." I stood up. "Do you, by any chance, have the blackmail notes, or did the cops take them?"

"I never told them about the notes. If something is happening under my nose, I'd rather handle it in-house than have authorities that aren't even supernatural putting their ugly noses in it. Even a hint of something like that could shut me down." Lisa stood and walked behind her desk. She rifled through one of the drawers and pulled out a manila envelope, handing it over. "Zhor had no idea who was behind it. Also in there is a list of the clients Zhor's had from the past two months."

Lisa was a fount of knowledge. I magicked the envelope to make it smaller and hid it in the inner jacket pocket. I didn't want anyone to know I had that kind of information. It made me a target in more ways than one.

"So, Mick used to come here a lot?" I asked as I backed toward the door. "Tell me about that," I requested with a smirk.

Chapter Five

We aren't discussing the murder, Mom," Gage told me when he answered the phone after my third time calling him. "I didn't kill Zhor, and I'm fine. I have an alibi, though that idiot cop told me I could have hired someone to do it for me."

The silent trick worked wonders on my middle child. I remained quiet while he vented, though he gave me no further helpful information on the murder or their relationship. Gage's tone was off when he spoke, and I knew he was upset, though I didn't push the issue. He'd come to me when he was ready. He always did.

I made a quick stop home because my instincts were screaming at me to go there, and I was glad. I found Gage sitting in my driveway, looking exhausted. I didn't call him on the lie he told by saying he was fine.

"Sorry, Mom. I should have told you I was here." Gage looked up at me with injured eyes. "Do you mind if I crash out here for a few days? Reporters are all over the place at home."

"You don't even have to ask, son. You could have let yourself in." I took his arm and helped him stand. "Go lay down and call if you need anything. I need to go to work and begin a case that I just started."

I said that because I knew he wanted to be left

alone. My motherly instincts told me to slay anyone close to my hurting child; however, I knew Gage wouldn't like that, and he handled things in his time. In his way, not mine. Gage hated it when I hovered like a helicopter. The best thing I could do was do what I needed to do with my day and be available when he needed me.

I set off for my office and called Chad on the way. Chad was eager to meet with me and said he'd meet me there. I stopped to put gas in my Jeep as I ran it a bit on the low side. It didn't take me a lot of extra time, but it did allow Chad a bit more to get to the office.

Still, I arrived ahead of him and was in the process of getting my office door unlocked when he pulled up. I waited in the hallway for him and hid a smile when I saw he was in uniform. He was either coming off a shift or about to start one.

"Heya, Chad. How's your day going?" I asked, holding the door for him.

"Not much has changed since I last talked to you," Chad hedged carefully, sliding past me. "I mean, it was only this morning. And boy am I glad that you called me; you work fast."

"Lip Service," I said to Chad as I crossed behind my desk. I did my best to keep my face deadpan.

The second my butt landed on my evil chair, everything collapsed. I barely missed having a cylinder in the hole where the sun doesn't shine. Parts when flying about the room like they grew wings as my derriere plopped not quite delicately onto the hard floor with a jolt. Chad shouted, jumped to his feet to see if I was okay, and got in the way of returning the chair to its host.

Chad fell face forward as it smacked him in the back, landing with his arms on either side of my hips and his face in my crotch. As he lifted his head with a chagrined grin, he watched the bastard of a chair reassemble itself and move out of the way.

"Well," Chad flushed, "at least you smell good. I don't know what just happened, but I am sorry, and I hope I didn't hurt you."

What the hell do you say to someone whose face landed between your legs and tells you that you smell good? Thanks didn't seem sufficient, and while the dirty part of my mind wanted to run with it, I mainly kept my mouth shut because Mick chose that moment to walk into my office and see Chad's questionable position between my legs.

Mick's eyes were a dangerous shade of yellow, and he grew three inches taller. Chad scrambled to his feet, reacting to the alpha power, even though he didn't know what that was. Mick strode across the room and plucked me from the floor like my chunkiness didn't exist. He set me gently on my feet, stuck his nose in my neck, and inhaled.

"If you pee on me, mutt, I swear we will have more issues than you can count on each paw," I warned Mick with a malevolent hiss.

"There's my girl," Mick murmured and swept his tongue across my neck. "The chair?" he asked casually now that he was under control and stepped away.

Chad nodded for me and shoved one of the plastic chairs my way, keeping his mouth shut as he watched the interplay between Mick and me. I moved a greater distance away, needing space. Mick was right. It was only a matter of time before we did each other in whatever way got us there quickest.

"What are you doing here?" my voice quivered in anticipation a little, and I hated that he noticed.

"I wanted to check on you and tell you that Gage isn't at his place." Mick flashed me a sexy smirk and wiggled his nose to let me know he could smell my

215

horniness.

"Gage is fine. He's at my house. If you don't mind, I need to have a meeting with my client that doesn't end with his face between my legs. At least, not until I'm paid," I shot a cocky smirk back at Mick when I saw his face flush with anger.

"It was unintentional, sir," Chad promised eagerly, ready to do anything to make Mick not angry at him.

"Don't worry about him," I waved off Mick. "He's leaving like a good dog."

I swore Mick's growl caused Chad to jump. I was amused at this, which made me a bitch, I'm sure. I ushered Mick out and locked the door behind him.

"Sorry about that." I wasn't sure what to say. Explaining that chair wasn't something quickly accomplished, and trying to verbalize the complicated relationship between Mick and me was damn near impossible.

"That is one smitten kitten, man," Chad joked uneasily. "Is he a cop? He's scary enough to be one."

"Not a cop, but Mick is a leader in this town." I felt tempted to tell Chad that Mick was the alpha of a wolf pack. I didn't, but damn I wanted to. "Let's get down to business, shall we?"

"Was I right? Did someone put a spell on me?" Chad's face pinkened with embarrassment.

"I hear you are quite the gardener and growing your own vegetable garden," I grinned. "Just think, you can make your own 'man'estrone, I mean, minestrone soup if you get horny enough. I'd have said stew, but you are lacking the meat." I was unquestionably terrible.

"I'd try to deny it, but I am sure that my face gives everything away. I take it that means that you know who did this to me?" Chad correctly guessed.

"I do," I nodded. "Next time you visit Lip Service, I

suggest it's with a heartfelt apology to the owner, who you called old. By the way, she's a demon. Never a good idea to insult the woman in charge of the people pleasuring you. That's how you end up with a garden salad in your pants for the rest of your life. Do you make your own dressing?"

"Oh, shit," Chad groaned at the ribbing. "Is it reversible?" His gulp was audible.

"With a sincere apology, Lisa will consider it. Come on," I joked. "You know the garden salad comment was funny. I'd offer to give you consolation head, but I think I'm the one that would be getting it in the form of cauliflower or broccoli."

Chapter Six

I pored over the list of names on the papers that Lisa gave me and started my research on each of the clients Zhor had seen. I hoped that I would see the town's newest resident, Wiley, on the list, but no such luck. I wondered if Gage knew that Zhor's side gig was a man-whore. That was a conversation for a different time.

I refocused and was able to eliminate over eighty percent of the people. It was the remaining twenty percent that had me floored. Some of the names weren't of residents from Glimmering Rock, and I was guessing that they lived in Branstone.

I called in a favor from Chad since he owed me for promising not to share his little secret garden and had him run searches on the people I couldn't find anything on online. Next, I swallowed my pride and asked Mick to come back to the office to see if he could offer any input.

The infuriating wolf couldn't have been very far away since he showed up in minutes, looking arrogant as all get out. It was hard when you were simultaneously wildly attracted to the man and wanted to strangle him to wipe the cocky look from his face.

"I love it when you need me," Mick told me in that smug voice that rankled my nerves. He plopped his large frame into the plastic chair and crossed an ankle over his knee.

I've seen this man in action. I knew that move was to draw my eyes to the snug way his jeans stretched over his junk. It worked, but I had the satisfaction of knowing why he did that.

Instead of tempting fate with my office chair again, I pulled the second plastic one over and slid the papers across my desk so he could see the narrowed-down list of names and not everything else.

"Do you recognize any of these names?" I asked Mick.

He took his time reading over each name and made a humming noise. I was about to lose my patience when I realized that he was communicating with his pack. I felt a flare of hope light in my chest, kept my cool, and held my tongue.

Only for as long as it took him to finish, pull my chair closer to his and ask, "What is the information worth to you?" Mick ran his hands up my thighs.

"Are you for real?" I blurted out. I was more annoyed than turned on. Mostly. "Here, I thought you were actually helping me."

"I am, sweetheart," Mick smirked at me, happy that he got under my skin. He tapped the paper on two names. "I know these two quite well. Is this about the murder?"

Damn the man. He'd know if I was lying, so I nodded my response and held my breath. Mick grew silent and appeared to be thinking about what he wanted to say. I resisted the urge to shake him and demand answers.

"Herb is a frequenter of the bar and Lip Service. We aren't that far apart, and he'd either come in before or after he visited Lisa's establishment. No, I'm not going to defend my going there either. Your face is easier to read than a mirror behind you while playing cards. We each have a past, and I don't hold that against you. However, I *do*

220

have something I'd like to hold against you." Mick waggled his eyebrows at me and licked his lips.

"I want to hate you," I groaned. "Keep talking. About Herb, not whatever innuendo you were about to make."

"Herb is a shady human. His scent is off, and something about him makes me want to rip his head off and use his skull as a candy bowl." Mick stopped talking and tapped his finger on my desk. "Some of the pack say he is dishonest, only not in those words. I was cleaning it up since I was in a lady's presence."

Mick didn't even have the decency to try and hide the shit-eating grin from his face as he said that. We both knew I was no lady. I wasn't going to dignify that with a response.

"Crowley said he cheats at pool, and on people," Mick finished. "Want me to dig further on him?"

"What about the other name?" I asked before answering. "And yeah, or point me in the direction I need to go to find out more."

"Kelly is just a fuck anything as much as possible type. He doesn't even try to hide it. I'd place wagers on Herb being the one that needs watching," Mick told me honestly. "I also feel obligated to say watch yourself around him. I've never seen him be dangerous before, but as I stated earlier, his scent is off."

Coming from Mick, it was a warning I would heed and take precautions. He knew my line of work and that I could handle a lot more than most people. His concern wasn't misplaced either since he's saved my bacon from the skillet a time or two.

"Noted, and thank you," I replied sincerely.

Chapter Seven

Armed with direction from Mick, I headed out the next day to Branstone. I was sure I had a tail on me, sent by the alpha, or it was Mick himself. I refused to look behind me to see or acknowledge that I knew someone was there. If I were honest with myself, I would admit that it was nice to have a backup. But I won't.

I found Herb's address quickly enough, and it wasn't too far away from where Gage lived. I knew Zhor had an apartment around here, but I wasn't sure of the exact location. I wouldn't be able to get near it anyway. The cops would still be crawling all over it.

Luckily, they knew nothing of the blackmail, or Herb and I would get to solve their case for them and rub their faces in it. Mick had gotten a picture of Herb from their security cameras, so I knew who I was looking for, and I scanned the faces around me, looking for the bald-headed slimeball. He wasn't an unattractive man, but I agreed with Mick; something wasn't right.

The mysterious blood running through my veins flowed a little faster, and my leprechaun genes kicked in because I saw Herb exiting his building as I approached. He was trying to blend into the crowd if I wasn't mistaken. He wore a pair of generic khakis and a faded red and blue plaid shirt; no imagination or pop to the wardrobe that would set him apart from anyone, right down to his well-worn loafers.

I followed at a distance, not that I was worried about being spotted. Herb had no idea who I was, and I had my hair shoved into a beanie to hide its changing nature. I didn't blend as well as he did, though I didn't stand out enough to draw a ton of attention either.

When Herb walked into one of those stores that sold sex toys, I dropped onto a bench outside a pharmacy and held back a laugh as my mind wandered. I liked how they put a pharmacy across from a sex store in case someone got the clap from dirty toys. They could get some meds to fix it on their way out of going back to complain and return the faulty toy. It was plausible as some were that dumb.

I didn't sit there long before Herb came back out with a brown paper bag clutched in his hand and began walking down the street. I got up and followed, keeping to the opposite side of the road. Half the time, I couldn't see the wolf who followed me. In my experience, even the best investigators could blow a lead by being too obvious, and even the utterly unaware people can spot a tail if they see them too many times.

I wasn't sure how observant Herb was, and I wanted to play it safe. I'd switch sides of the street in a couple of blocks if he went into another store. It was too hard for me to tell where he headed right now, other than more into town, away from Glimmering Rock, Lip Service, and Mick's bar.

Following Herb, I witnessed him leer at over twenty women and fourteen men in one hour. I saw Herb take intrusive photos, write things down in a notebook he kept hidden in his pocket, and make inappropriate comments to people of all ages. He got shot down by eight people he propositioned and stole food from sidewalk displays

224

and vendors.

With grudging respect, I had to admit that when Mick was right, he was right. I had very little doubt that Herb was the man behind the blackmail letters. Given his aggressive nature, he might even be who killed Zhor. I just needed to find evidence to support that thought.

Now would be the perfect time for me to sneak a peek into his apartment since he was outside annoying innocent people with his used car, snake oil salesman vibe. I turned around and headed back the way I'd been traveling and kicked my walking speed up a notch.

I briefly considered letting Lisa know that I had a solid lead. However, I wanted concrete proof before providing information that might cause her to go off the rail on a human city. Plus, if he were the murderer, I'd need to let the police know so that they got off Gage's case, and mine too.

I didn't often use magic in the human city, though I would need to get his door open this time. I knew I had a tail since Mick all but told me I would, so if things got out of hand, I'd have help. I also needed to be careful not to attract the attention of the Branstone police since they'd questioned me only yesterday. Breaking and entering wouldn't look good and might possibly put me in the spotlight for Zhor's untimely demise.

Fifteen minutes later, I made it to Herb's apartment building and was fortunate enough to catch another tenant walking out the locked front door and sliding in behind them. I cataloged the lobby as I searched for the elevator and finally found one with an out-of-order sign on the door. That sucked.

I opened the door to the stairs by leaning into it, began the hike up five flights, and got halted on the third level. I might have been out of breath, but all oxygen fled my lungs when I saw Danny staring at me. My cheating ex.

"Risa, what are you doing here?" Danny looked me up and down with a longing look on his handsome face.

"Working. What the hell are you doing?" I snapped, trying to ignore the pang in my heart.

"I have a client here that I was helping." Danny took a defensive stance which told me the client was a female.

Without warning, he backed me into the stairwell corner, caged my head, and kissed me. I'd forgotten how good he was at that and how it turned me on. Yet, I couldn't help compare the heat to the reactions Mick brought out in me. Mick's fire was far hotter, though Danny was just as effective as getting the juices flowing.

Regardless, he'd cheated on me, which was front and center in my mind. I didn't care what circumstances he'd been in; it still happened. I pushed Danny away, my temper sparking.

"I didn't give you permission for that," I growled angrily. "You lost those privileges. If you don't mind, I have work to do."

I shoved past him, and the exit would have been so much more powerful if I hadn't tripped over my foot, had my toe catch the end of the stair, and pitched forward, landing boob first on the cement stairs. Not my most graceful move.

Ignoring Danny's questions about my welfare, I pushed myself up and kept walking up the stairs until I got to Herb's floor. With a careful look behind me to make sure Danny hadn't followed, I opened the door with my jacketed elbow and entered the corridor.

Non-descript doors and carpet greeted me, and I quietly strode down the hall, looking at apartment numbers. No one looked outside, questioned me, or what I was doing here, all things I took as both good and bad signs.

I stopped in front of Herb's door and let some of my

magic loose, which popped open the lock, and I used my foot to push the door open. Fingerprints wouldn't be a good thing for me to leave behind. I stepped gingerly into the stale-smelling apartment and let the door swing closed behind me.

Chapter Eight

Time was of the essence, and I didn't want to be in Herb's apartment longer than I needed to. I mean, considering I wasn't supposed to be here at all, leaving as quickly as possible seemed like a good idea.

The apartment was a disaster. Empty takeout containers stacked on the kitchen counter, cupboard doors left open showing unused dishes, glasses, and boxed food with expired dates. There were porn DVDs strewn about a tissue-covered coffee table, gross; I touched nothing.

I moved to the bedroom and saw a variety of toys, lubrication, and more tissues. I backed out of there as fast as humanly possible. So far, I hadn't seen anything that stuck out to me, and there was only the bathroom and a room with a closed-door left. No wonder Herb was single.

Ignoring the bathroom, I used a little more magic to open the closed door and saw an office—an old desktop computer perched on a beat-up wooden desk. Papers haphazardly stacked on one corner, pictures on another.

I moved to look closer at the photos and saw several of Lisa inside Lip Service. Apparently, she wasn't aware that her picture had been taken, though none of them showed anything that would put her or her business in peril.

I wasn't knowledgeable enough to break into his

computer, and I didn't want to try and see if it was password protected right now. I had no clue what my timeline in this pit would be and didn't want to chance discovery.

I used the toe of my boot to tug at the drawer handles and was surprised when they opened easily. The bottom drawer contained manila file folders, and I figured this was where the gold was located.

I dug into my pockets and pulled out a pair of latex gloves. I had a moment of distraction where Danny's kiss haunted me, and I got sidetracked. The sound of feet snapped me out of my trance, and I dropped into a squat to make myself a smaller target.

There was no door opening sound, and I relaxed a slight bit. While I was down there, I put the gloves on and rifled through the folders. I saw several files that contained random photos, then came across one with Zhor.

I pulled it out and found more images of the satyr and Lisa. Interesting. There were no documents to explain, just the photos. I pulled one picture out to look closer and saw Zhor intimately close with someone, his hand sliding something into the pocket of whoever he was with the moment the image got captured.

I frowned and studied the picture closer. It was inside Lip Service. I recognized the waiting room area where Lisa had clients meet with their prospective partners for the next hour. I pulled out another photo, a few more, and saw the same pattern. On the backs were scrawled dates, all within the past six months. But why was Herb so concerned with what or who Zhor was doing?

To further that point, what *was* Zhor doing? I grabbed my phone from my pocket and snapped pictures of the photos before replacing them in the file. I went through the other files, looked for documents, and found some handwritten music scores.

230

I gently removed them from the folder and looked through them. I found Zhor's name scrawled at the top by the third sheet. These must be songs we wrote for his performances at the club he played at when I first met him. Why did Herb have them? I took pictures of those as well and kept searching. I didn't find anything else noteworthy to Zhor or Lisa and moved on to the next drawers.

There was enough in these drawers to cast shadows over Herb's life concerning Zhor, and I planned on letting Chad know. I found a scrawled piece of paper in the top drawer with the restaurant's name that Gage worked at as a chef. My protective instincts roared to the surface.

"Risa," Mick's voice startled me so badly I fell backward and cracked my head on the window sill. "Time to go."

There was no time for me to react. Mick had the window opened and had bodily shoved me through it to a very narrow fire escape before he climbed out after me and shut the window.

"What the hell?" I hissed at the aggravated wolf-man.

"Herb is on his way up the stairs," Mick pushed me to crawl down the ladder. "Didn't figure you wanted to get caught inside."

Mick wasn't wrong, and I didn't want to admit it. Yet, I still moved as quickly and quietly as I could down the rusty squeaking fire escape that didn't look strong enough to hold both of us simultaneously.

Once we hit the lowest section, Mick jumped straight down to the ground and held his arms out for me to jump. I hesitated only a moment, more concerned with being caught than I was about crushing the man who'd just saved my ass.

I dropped and landed with Mick's arms around my waist as if he expended no effort, leaving me breathless.

231

What strange power did this man have over me to cause these reactions that I didn't welcome? Despite the warning bells in my head, I crushed my lips to his.

Mick rapidly backed me up and thudded my back on the apartment building wall with force as he devoured my mouth. Yeah, I was the bitch who compared the kisses I'd received less than thirty minutes apart, and the answer didn't make me happy. I didn't stop the kiss right away, though. I mean, come on, that kind of magic is worth it.

With tingly body parts and swollen lips, I pushed Mick away and dropped to my feet after I unwound my legs from around his waist. I had no idea when that happened.

"Herb has photos of Zhor and Lisa, among others, and he had the name of Gage's restaurant written on a piece of paper," I blurted out in a breathy whisper.

"Walk," Mick demanded, dragging me behind him as we exited the alley.

Chapter Nine

I sat behind the wheel of my beloved Jeep and fumed. Mick had all but thrown me into the front seat and disappeared. I only liked being manhandled when in the heat of the moment, which was not what that moment was.

I started the Jeep and drove back to Glimmering Rock. My first stop would be to see Lisa. It didn't take me long; I might have sped, hard to say. I admit to nothing. Especially wound-up hormones that left me wanting. Nope, nothing to confess here.

Walking into Lip Service to talk with a succubus when frustrated and turned on might not have been the best of choices. Lisa practically leaped on me when I entered.

"Girl, you are a walking beacon for my powers," Lisa purred. "God, it tastes delicious, and damn, do you need to get laid."

"Okay, can we focus on why I'm here?" I pursed my lips. "Are you familiar with a guy named Herb?"

"Sure am," Lisa scowled. "He's a douche. A couple of people here were his favorites, Zhor being one of them." Lisa pointed to an elf-like waif across the room, "Phoebe is another. Why?"

"I found several photos of you and Zhor in his

desk." I pulled out my phone and showed her the pictures. "They were all taken here, and I'm guessing that you didn't know you were the subject. My next question is, what is Zhor doing?"

Lisa enlarged the image on the screen and studied it closely, and then yanked me down the hall after her toward her office. That was the third time today someone pushed me around, and it grated on my nerves.

"I can walk on my own, thank you," I snapped and wrenched out of her powerful grip on my arm.

Lisa cocked an eyebrow at me, gestured for me to enter her office, and then slammed the door behind us. She flounced to her chair behind her desk and flipped her blonde locks haughtily.

"Each person employed here has to sign a non-disclosure and a non-compete. Each of those was a regular client until not too long ago when they suddenly stopped coming here," Lisa ground out. "If I had to guess, it appears that Zhor was moonlighting and trying to steal clients, so he didn't have to pay me the house cut. Hardly seems worth blackmail, but it pisses me the hell off."

"What if Herb wasn't after Zhor but was instead after you?" I suggested. "There were just as many photos of you as there were Zhor. Were you two ever involved?"

Lisa let out a bellowing laugh. "I slept with him," Lisa confirmed. "We didn't date. I like to sample the goods before employing someone. If they can get me off, I don't need to worry about unsatisfied clients."

That was a hell of a perk, I thought. I scooted forward and put a plan into play with Lisa for later that night to see if we could trap Herb. I left Lip Service with an outfit tucked under my arm and went home to prepare.

A couple of hours later, I stopped back at Lip Service to pick Lisa up, and we drove to Herb's apartment, where I let us into the building again. Thankfully there was no

Danny on the stairs this time, and our entrance onto the fifth floor was without event.

I knocked on Herb's door while Lisa remained out of sight, but her power was in full swing. It was highly uncomfortable to be so turned on with someone so icky. However, it was in the interest of getting answers. I'd deal.

Herb answered and flicked his eyes over me with a slick look. I didn't even need to look down to know he was ready to go at a moment's notice. He didn't utter a word, just held the door open for me to enter.

Herb was so intent on staring at my barely clad ass that he didn't shut the door behind him, leaving Lisa room to enter behind him. When Herb's hands came in contact with my upper thigh and lower butt cheeks, I spun and pinned him to the wall with one hand around his throat. The other twisted his balls until he screeched out with the remaining oxygen in his lungs.

Lisa employed her seductive powers, this I knew because I felt it down to my bones. I don't know what visuals she presented to Herb's mind, but he begged for mercy, release, everything. He confessed to every last thing he'd ever done in his lifetime, including stalking Lisa and blackmailing Zhor for information about Lisa.

That ten minutes felt like a lifetime, never getting a happy ending with a man. I had my legs squeezed shut and was terrified to move until Lisa backed off using her succubus magic. I was sweating and damp in several places and aching for release.

As if Mick knew, he appeared in the doorway as we turned to leave, his eyes flashing yellow dangerously as he tried to keep his wolf caged. I don't know if it was Lisa at work or not, but I went to him voluntarily.

Me, wearing nothing but an almost transparent, low cut, short hemmed slinky dress and heels that no woman should ever have to walk on. Mick wasted zero time picking me up and throwing me over his shoulder caveman-style, leaving me a view of his perfect backside. I looked up at Lisa as Mick carried me away, and the woman winked at me.

Maybe it was the fresh air once we got outside, but I came to my senses and halted Mick's movements.

"Hey, I need to contact Chad," I practically whispered. "You know, the guy's face that was in my crotch yesterday." Somewhere behind me, I heard Lisa's delighted laughter.

"Risa, never change!" Lisa shouted her encouragement to me. "You might have some succubus blood in you. Bring him to his knees!"

"I swear, sweetheart, if that man's face comes anywhere near that hemline, he will be wolf chow," Mick growled, sliding me down the hardened front of him. "Don't think I didn't smell Danny on you earlier. My wolf doesn't do jealousy well."

I reached between us and slid my phone from my bra. I fiddled with some of the apps on the screen, sent the recording of Herb's confessions to Chad, and then called him.

"Hey, handsome," I replied when Chad answered. "I just sent you a message. Do whatever you need to do to bring this to a happy ending." I purposely worded my conversation to goad Mick. I knew he could hear both sides of the conversation, but he didn't know that Chad caught on to my little word game and played along.

"There are always happy endings when you are involved, Risa. Oh, and by the way, my gardening days are over," Chad revealed huskily. "I don't expect to hear anything back for at least a day or two on whatever information I pass on. Those detectives are a tight knit group and don't like outsider opinions much. But I promise to find a way to leak the information to them. It'll be a good night for me, hopefully you find your own garden to play in."

I hung up the phone and ran my fingers over Mick's chin, down his neck, and kept going until I stopped on the button of his jeans. Mick emitted that low growl that drove me wild, his eyes hot on mine.

"You know what, puppy-dog? I think I'd like to learn a little about wolf-style," I taunted. I couldn't believe I was doing this. It might be the biggest mistake of my life, but I wanted him. "Take me home." I cupped his junk on the wild chance that he didn't get the innuendo. "I can offer some lip service."

About the Author

Michelle Lee is a Pacific Northwest native with a mind open to possibilities. Growing up, people often saw her with her face buried in a book and not much has changed. She's living her life dream of writing books that set her imagination free and explore the possibilities and mysteries she sees in the land all around her.

Find novel-length works by Michelle and additional *I S.P.I.* installments at:

www.BlueForgePress.com

www.ingramcontent.com/pod-product-compliance
Lightning Source LLC
Chambersburg PA
CBHW070526100726
7907CB00004B/1004